THE LAST MAN

DEVLIN THRILLER NO.3

JAMES CARVER

1

The old man peered over his half-moon glasses. He wore a blue striped bowling shirt. His liver-spotted hands rested on a glass display cabinet. Below his fleshy forearms lay rows of glittering rings, watches, and broaches, all set into a burgundy velvet cloth. He was tracking the movements of his only customer, a boy of fifteen at most, who was pretending to browse.

"Can I help you, son?"

"Uh, yeah... Maybe..."

The boy was stick-thin, and tall, with a backpack hanging off his shoulder. He looked nervous, moved awkwardly, and wore a fleece-lined denim jacket over a red flannel shirt, both of which were too big for him. The cuffs of the jacket were blackened with dirt and matched his fingernails. He scanned the shop and flinched when he saw the CCTV cameras hanging from the ceiling.

"I... I got something I wanted to sell... for cash."

"Okay." The old man beckoned him over with the flick of a hand. The boy approached the counter and pulled a white handkerchief out of his jacket pocket which he laid on the glass. Teasing away the folds of the cloth, he revealed a thick gold band with a coat of arms etched onto its oval face.

The old man picked it up and twirled it around in his fat fingers. He took an eyeglass out of the breast pocket of his bowling shirt, gave the ring a brief once over, and put it back down on the handkerchief.

"Thirty dollars."

"Wha...? Thirty?"

"We got a lot of gold rings. They sell but I won't make much more than fifty on it, if I have to sell, which I think we both know I will."

"But it's solid gold. Aren't you gonna weigh it?"

"Listen, kid, I've been doing this job since before you were born and I wouldn't give more than thirty for this piece."

"It's worth more than that. I'll take it somewhere else."

"Fine. That's your choice. But the other places around here, they will ask for ID. Maybe they already have. You got ID?"

The boy didn't answer.

"Didn't think so. How old are you?"

"Eighteen."

"Eighteen... Sure. You're eighteen and you don't have ID." The old man shrugged. "I don't know where this ring is from, if it's hot..."

"It's an heirloom."

"An heirloom?"

"My uncle won it as a prize. He played lawn bowls."

"Lawn bowls? Jeez. Well, it's original, I'll give you that." The old man picked up the ring and peered at it again, this time with his naked eye. "It doesn't look sporty. The inscription on the face looks like a coat of arms." He looked back up at the boy with his moist, colorless eyes. "I shouldn't have even let you into the shop but I can see you need money so I'm giving you the benefit of the doubt. Thirty's a good offer, you should take it."

The boy thought about it. While he wrestled with himself over what to do, a younger man entered the shop. He was dark, short, and wore a skin-tight black v-neck t-shirt over his broad, worked-out body. He nodded at the old man, went behind the counter, and dabbed a code into a wall-mounted key-lock. A door clicked open and he disappeared into the back of the shop.

"Okay. Thirty," said the boy.

"You sure?"

"I'm sure."

The old guy started to ring up the cash register.

"Hold on," said the boy. He swung his backpack down on the counter, unzipped it, and pulled out a plastic bag.

"What's this?"

"There's another dozen rings in the bag."

The old man took the bag and stared into it.

"Your uncle ever thought of going professional?"

In the back of the shop, the man in the v-neck watched the CCTV feed from the front of the shop. He watched his father write out a ticket and hand over a wad of bills to the boy. The boy, who looked like hadn't had a wash or seen a bed in a week, took the bills and pushed them into his pants pocket.

The boy left and the man in the v-neck got up and went back out front.

"I gotta head out, Pop."

"You just got here."

"I can't remember if I locked my car. Back in five."

IT HADN'T BEEN the first pawn shop the boy had tried but it was the first to make him an offer. He knew he'd been ripped off, but now he had nearly four hundred dollars stuffed in his pocket he could eat again. It was two days since he'd last had anything; a ham roll and Doritos from a Best Buy that left him with small change. Hunger ate at him like a disease. Hunger inside of him, cold outside of him. It was mid-November and frost glistened on the sidewalk. He pulled up his fleece-lined collar, dug his hands into his flimsy gray sweatpants, and walked four blocks until he found a Honey Dew Donuts store. All he wanted was a maple pancake sausage sandwich before he collapsed, but he had to think straight. The money from the pawn shop was rolled up in his pocket and he needed to ration it, separate out what he required for day-to-day things.

He turned down a narrow side-road into a small courtyard surrounded by apartment blocks. He checked no one was around and crouched by the wall to open his backpack. Then he froze. A car had come to an abrupt halt and parked right up on the sidewalk so that it blocked off the entrance.

The owner of the car, a black Audi sedan, got out and stood at the entrance to the courtyard. The boy recognized him as the younger man from the pawn shop.

"Hey, you," shouted the man. He pointed at the boy, his wrist and fingers ringed with heavy gold jewelry.

The boy zipped up his backpack and stood.

"You sold us stolen goods, kid."

"No... They were..."

"Shut up. You're a criminal and I want my money back."

"It's my money. The man in the shop took my rings."

"He's an old man and you preyed on him."

"No. I swear."

"Don't lie to me. Give me the rings. They're stolen and I'm reporting you to the cops."

"I'm not an idiot."

"What did you say?"

"You're lying..." The boy's heart was beating hard and blood pumped up and down his fatigued body. Hungry, tired, and wired, he felt his anger rising, spiraling.

"What did you say?" repeated the man in the v-neck. He stood only a couple of feet away from him and the boy could see just how worked out he was. Bull necked, his barrel chest squashed into his black top.

"You're not going to give the rings to the cops," said the kid. "You're just gonna take the money because you think you can... Because I'm..."

The boy didn't finish his sentence because the other man had punched him in the side of his neck. His legs gave way instantly and he found himself on the ground, the high apartment buildings swirling around him. Dimly, as if it were happening to someone else, he felt his pockets being searched. The anger that had been blooming within him now became a force of its own. He realized his hand was resting on something, an object, hard and square. He grabbed it and swung it in a wild arc. Though he hardly knew what he was doing, the object in his hand connected with something and splintered in two. The boy sat up and saw that the man in the v-neck was reeling back, sitting on the paving-stones and clutching his head. He wasn't making a sound.

The boy stood, his head pounding, half-a-brick in his hand, brick dust in his mouth. The other man was covered in blood, rocking back and forth, and the boy felt a sudden rush of terror. He dropped the brick, picked up his backpack, and looked around. The courtyard was quiet. The windows of the apartments were empty. If anyone had been watching, they hadn't made themselves known.

He climbed over the hood of the Audi and landed back in the high street drenched in a cold terror. How badly had he hurt the man? What if he died? He'd be a murderer. And he'd be a murderer for the rest of his life.

They were right, he thought. They knew what he was and they were right. He was evil. There was a demon inside him, just like they had said. Worse than that, maybe he wanted to have that demon inside him. Maybe he had let it in in the first place.

2

I t was late afternoon and getting dark. A murky winter dark. They'd been walking around the theme park since ten in the morning. The kids were still excited and wanted to see and do more. It was wonderful and wearying.

"You okay, Sarah?"

"Yeah, I'm okay."

"I know the kids can be too much."

"Oh, let them be too much. They cheer me up. It's why I came with you guys. I'm really grateful you invited me."

Sarah Wilson had come to Edaville Theme Park for a change of scene, and in the hopes that being with her sister Theresa and her nieces would lift her spirits. And it had. But still, it had been a long day. They'd been on every ride in the park, a few more than once, but mostly they'd waited in line. Now, not being the one legally responsible for the children, she was itching for a break, some time to be alone. And she felt guilty for it. If she was tired of the children and she wasn't even a mother, Lord knows how Theresa felt. Even so, Theresa had noticed Sarah wilting and didn't appear to mind, or if she did, she hid it very well.

"You go have a walk round by yourself. Get yourself a grown-up drink maybe. They want another go on the crane drop and the wait is at least half an hour."

"Well..."

"Go on. Take some time. It's an order."

"Okay. I'll meet you over by the Candy Depot and get some treats for the girls."

"Sounds great."

Sarah found a hot drinks kiosk, bought herself a pumpkin spice latte, and then went browsing in the gift shops searching for some warmth rather than something to buy.

The fairground lights were bright and the people milling around her were happy. Though it was a relief to be by herself, it also brought all the sadness back, brought back the stark difference between her life a couple of weeks ago and her life now. Just over a fortnight ago, she had still been in a five-year relationship and a large, lovingly furnished three-bedroom apartment. In the space of seven days, all of that had fallen apart. The contrast in her life before and after those seven days sometimes caused her to stop whatever she was doing and stand still, paralyzing her in numb wonder.

Theresa and the girls, as much as she loved them, were also an uncomfortable reminder of where she wasn't in her life, and where she thought she might have been getting to.

She wandered out of the gift shop area and mooched for a while, sipping at her latte to make it last, and set about finding a bench to rest her feet. Instead, she spotted something quite unexpected, at least unexpected in a theme park built for families. It was a sign for a psychic.

The sign was a green-painted finger on a yellow background. It pointed the way toward a small cabin in a corner of the fairground. The cabin had two windows on either side of the door. Sheer drapes hung in the windows and a sign on the door read,

"Mystical Solutions. Amber Luna. Medium, Author, and Psychic. Twenty-five dollars for a 30-minute consultation."

Sarah had never visited a psychic before. Her settled view was that they were all frauds. Yet, standing there now, holding her spiced latte and wondering what her once certain future had to offer, she decided *to hell with it.*

You only live once, she thought. *Unless you're a Buddhist.*

Maybe she should give mediums a chance to prove themselves, she reasoned. After all, Amber Luna couldn't be any more wrong about Sarah's future than Sarah had been herself. And at worst it was half an hour of entertainment.

Sarah opened the cabin door and stepped into a small empty waiting room with a table, two small couches, and a whirring electric heater. Soft focus pictures hung on the wall, all of them featuring a heavily made-up woman with big, dark-brown hair. The kind of hairdo Elizabeth Taylor or Joan Collins favored in the seventies and eighties. The photos were either of the woman looking directly into the camera, or of her 'at work,' sitting across a table from a client.

A wooden wall with a door in the middle cut the cabin in half, and from behind the door Sarah heard two voices. One of the voices, the dominant voice, was steady and calm. The other was much higher and choked with emotion. The emotional voice became gradually higher until it trembled and broke into sobs. It was at that moment when Sarah seriously doubted whether or not she was doing the right thing, and almost turned on her heels and left. But she was in a funny kind of mood, a-once-in-a-lifetime-kind-of-mood, open to whatever might be thrown at her. Most of all, Sarah was desperate for change.

There were more sobs from the other side of the wall, some snuffling, and then the calm voice again. Then silence followed by breezy social chat, thank-yous, and goodbyes. The door opened and a woman in her sixties wearing a pink blouse and chiffon scarf came out. A slightly younger woman — the one in the pictures on the wall with the big Liz Taylor hair — followed behind, looking sympathetic. The older woman dabbed her eyes with a ball of scrunched tissue, then they embraced.

"Thank you, Amber."

"Not at all. Take care of yourself, Kitty."

The older lady left and Amber turned to Sarah.

"Hello. Are you here for a consultation?"

"I am. If you have a spot available. I didn't need to make a reservation, did I?"

"No. That's fine. I was about to shut up for the day but I'm more than happy to see one more client. Step this way... Sorry, I didn't get your name."

"Sarah. My name's Sarah."

"Very pleased to meet you, Sarah. I'm Amber."

The preamble into the consultation was quick. Introductions were made and the money was paid by card. Then the two women settled into two armchairs facing each other in a space so small it imposed a sense of intimacy. The consultation room was lit by one low-watt desk lamp covered in a fine red cloth. Though it was dark, Sarah noticed framed quotes on the wall from Einstein, Ram Dass, Deepak Chopra, and other names she didn't recognize.

It was surprisingly quiet, thought Sarah, given the cabin was made entirely from wood. She could hear the fairground noises outside, but it was faint and mostly she just heard the whirr of an electric heater.

"You're tense," said Amber, looking at Sarah with a motherly concern.

"Uh... Oh, sure. Yes, I guess I am." Sarah was cradling her spiced latte in her mittened hands and sitting upright, not giving in to the softness of the armchair. "This is my first... consultation."

Amber leaned over and placed a hand on Sarah's arm. "It's all going to be absolutely fine. I take the best care of my clients, who are my sole and primary concern. There's really nothing to worry about."

Amber removed her hand and laid it on the table. She breathed in deeply, then exhaled for several seconds, like she was 'tuning in'.

"I'm feeling more than tension coming through, though," Amber said with a frown.

"Really?"

"Yes. I get a very strong sense that there's been an event. A big event in your life."

Sarah sighed inwardly. It was, she supposed, predictable that a woman in her mid-thirties turning up by herself for a physic reading might have experienced some kind of 'event' or other.

"Like the ending of a relationship?" Amber added.

"Uh, well, yeah... That... Yeah."

"I can see that it's been a hard transition. But you must know this one thing; it's absolutely for the best."

"Okay."

"But I can see another shadow. A shadow from the past... A..."

Sarah raised a hand suddenly. "Wait. I don't mean to be rude, but can we *not* do the past?"

This request seemed to irritate Amber, and she looked perplexed.

"It's just that I'm not that interested in the past," Sarah continued. "In fact, I've had enough of the past. I really want to know about the future. What does my future look like?"

"Well, that's quite a broad question."

"Sure. I appreciate that. But ever since the end of the... 'big event,' I'm all about the future. Anything you can give me on that would be great."

Amber nodded her big hairdo and smiled. Distant voices and laughter from theme park visitors came through the thin walls and the heater droned.

"Any particular aspects of the future? Anything you'd particularly like to know about?"

Sarah considered the question for a moment. "What about, where will I be in five years' time? Is that specific enough?"

Amber settled back into her chair and gazed at a point somewhere over Sarah's head.

"Where will you be in five years' time?" she repeated to herself. Then there followed a long stretch of silence before Amber spoke again. "I see a path bending away, bending away from the path you thought you were on only recently. I see you changing your career." She looked directly at Sarah. "At the moment you're in a career in which you look after people."

Okay, not too shabby, thought Sarah. Even if she was a fraud, she was a good fraud. Sarah might actually get her twenty-five dollars' worth. "Yeah, I am."

"I can definitely see a major career change coming. To something more personal, one-on-one, something in the field of counseling... psychology, well-being."

That's quite a large field, thought Sarah.

Amber then spoke for a while, painting a future with generalities and platitudes that left plenty of room for interpretation. While she spoke, she threw out leading statements and open-ended questions. Yet, Sarah didn't bite and said very little, and as the half-hour ended Amber's energy was fading. The self-proclaimed psychic seemed to realize she was fighting a losing battle with a skeptic and so she brought Sarah's reading to an abrupt close.

"I see our time's up," she said through a fixed smile.

"Oh, yes... Well, thank you."

"I hope you found the consultation helpful."

"Well, sure, a bit..."

"You know, I do feel that your energy is very... How shall I put it? Blocked."

"Well, I wouldn't say that. I'm just someone who's naturally —"

A loud thud stopped Sarah mid-sentence. Something had fallen to the floor, but in the low light of the room it was difficult to see what it was. Both women, a little startled, looked around for the cause of the sound.

"What was that?" Sarah asked.

"I think it was a frame coming off its picture hook. I'm sorry if it gave you a shock."

"Uh, no... It's okay. Well, thank you, Amber. That was very enlight —"

And then it happened again. Another thud. Another object had fallen to the floor and this time Sarah saw it was one of the framed quotes.

Sarah looked at Amber Luna who was sitting erect in her chair.

"My goodness, but the walls here are very thin," Amber said sharply. "They can't even hold a picture."

"Yeah. Or the picture hooks weren't put in right."

Then a third framed picture fell, and then the fourth and the fifth. And the pictures kept on falling until the walls were bare.

The two women sat very still and for a moment didn't speak or hardly breathe.

"Is there some kind of earthquake?" asked Sarah.

Amber had a hand braced against her ample bosom and looked genuinely terrified.

"No. It's no earthquake. I think... I think it's some kind of... spiritual energy..."

"Spiritual energy? Are you kidding me?"

"No. I am most certainly not."

Sarah's expression shifted from shock to cynicism. "Okay. Right. I get it. Wow. I gotta hand it to you, I don't know how you did that... What is it? Fishing wire? Is that it? Is there an accomplice outside pushing the hooks? When you get someone you think is 'blocked' you pull this trick? Is that it?"

"No... No, I didn't do anything. I swear to you."

Sarah had to admit, either Amber was a very good actor or she really did look like she was telling the truth. The blood had drained from her face and her eyes had widened in horror. She was clutching the sides of her armchair as if it were about to take off, and was gaping like she might have a cardiac arrest. But she wasn't looking at the suddenly bare walls now. She was staring right at Sarah as if she had seen the devil himself.

"Are you okay ?" asked Sarah nervously.

"No," Amber gasped. "No. I'm not. Your face..."

Sarah suddenly felt very cold, shockingly cold. A coldness that was more than an absence of heat. It was more like an absence of love.

"What about my face?"

"There's someone else there..."

"What?... Shut-up. Shut up right now... You're actually scaring me..."

"It's true, I can see it. I can see another face in your face... it's like there's someone else hiding inside you..."

Sarah shot up from her chair.

"This isn't cool, lady. It isn't cool at all. In fact, what you're doing, it's despicable and maybe illegal." She turned and pulled the door open. The glass pane in a picture frame cracked beneath her feet as light poured in from the waiting room. Without looking back, Sarah rushed out into the crisp winter air and the company of hundreds of strangers teeming through the theme park.

She strode away from the dusty old hut, as far away from

that con artist as possible. *That was one hell of a setup,* she thought, feeling terribly upset and her heart racing. The old lady must reserve it for people like Sarah. Real skeptics who didn't get taken in. Then she thought about how cold it got in there, icy, as if all the warmth had been sucked out of her body. How could she have made that happen? But then Sarah remembered the electric heater and how, now she thought about it, she was sure it had stopped droning at the end of the session. That must be it, of course, Amber kicked a switch under the table. Or something like that. *What a fake. With a name like Amber Luna, what else had I expected.*

Sarah heard her name and a whistle. Theresa and her nieces were sitting on a bench eating hot dogs. She fixed a smile on her face and went to greet them.

The girls had ketchup round their mouths and were swinging their legs up and down.

"We went on the crane drop again, Aunt Sarah," said Amy through a half-chewed hot-dog

"You did? Was it good?"

"Yeah. It was great, wasn't it Mom?"

"Yeah. Even better than the first and second time. How 'bout you Aunt Sarah? What did you get up to?"

"Me?" said Sarah, looking back toward Amber Luna's shed. "Oh, I just had a pumpkin spice latte."

"Was it nice?"

"I've had better."

3

Father Devlin's first wedding at Holy Cross was turning out to be an education. The groom's suit was a slick affair, shiny and skin-tight, more suited to a nightclub than a wedding. His red hair was shaved completely at the sides, and combed back in a mound at the crown with what must have been a bucket of hair gel. His face, lined from cigarettes and sun, was prematurely aged, making him look at least ten years older than he was. His name was Callum Driscoll and he belonged to a local family that had plenty of money to throw about.

The bride was small and demur, and wore a designer dress of some kind. It was flashy and embellished with clusters of crystals that sparkled whenever she moved.

The preparations for the ceremony had been handled by Father O'Neil. Devlin had taken over at the last minute when O'Neil was too ill to continue his duties. O'Neil hadn't given Devlin any kind of briefing and it hadn't started well. Only minutes before the service, the father of the groom, a thug in a suit called Tony Driscoll, had asked Devlin if they could change the vows. He had produced a scrap of paper and a hundred dollar bill.

"Not without getting the Pope on the phone," Devlin had replied, gently pushing the paper and the money away.

Driscoll had growled under his breath but didn't push it. Even he understood the day required some kind of decorum.

Devlin finished the service with the words; '... go in peace to glorify the Lord with your life,' and watched the Recessional begin with the couple proceeding back down the aisle and out of the church.

Among the scant instructions O'Neil had left was a note informing Devlin that he would be required to attend the wedding reception at an upscale restaurant in Boston. Devlin took the note literally. He drove to the restaurant, and took his seat at the top table with the couple and their parents. He listened to the speeches and raised a glass of orange juice to the toasts. But as soon as the last toast had been made and the glasses had hit the table, Devlin made his excuses to the table, rose, and left.

He'd only made it to the door when he felt a hand on his shoulder. He turned to see Tony Driscoll scowling back at him, already steaming with booze. Right from the get-go, he'd been sinking pints of Guinness followed by whiskey chasers.

"Where d'you think you're going?" barked Driscoll over the wedding band playing 'Fly Me To the Moon.'

"I have a meeting back at the church."

"I was promised by Father O'Neil that he'd stay the whole evening."

"I'm not Father O'Neil."

Driscoll frowned, then he smiled like he'd suddenly got the measure of Devlin. He dug into his pants pocket, pulled out a clip of bills, and began thumbing them.

"No," said Devlin. "There's been a misunderstanding. I do have pressing business and I don't take money. Ever."

Driscoll stopped smiling and put his money away. "You know

what I think? I think you think you're too good for us. I saw it in your face the moment I met you. You think my family isn't good enough for you or your church? Well, let me tell you something you should already know. I give a lot of money to the Holy Cross. A lot of money. So, you already took money from me the day you started there as a priest."

"Thank you for your generous and selfless donations through the proper channels, Mr. Driscoll. The church welcomes everyone. God welcomes everyone. I couldn't be happier to have married your son and his wife, and been at the start of their life together. I just don't take money personally. And by the way, if you ever come up from behind and lay your hand on my shoulder again you had better be prepared for a different kind of conversation."

"Screw you, I'd knock your holy ass into next week." The band was getting into full stride forcing Driscoll to raise his voice. "Get out of my reception, you clown."

As Devlin drove back to the Holy Cross rectory he turned the events of the wedding over in his head. He was still wondering what else O'Neil might have neglected to tell him about when he ran into his next surprise. He slotted his key into the rectory door lock and noticed that a small patch of paint by the deadbolt had been scraped away completely. It looked recent and the exposed wood beneath was still a healthy pale yellow. He was also pretty sure it hadn't been that way yesterday.

"Everything okay, Father?"

Devlin turned to see the new sexton, a man called Hoyt Tanner, watching Devlin with interest. Gusts of wind and spots of rain swept over the two men.

"The paint on the door," said Devlin. "It's come off. And there's some damage to the frame."

The sexton peered over Devlin's shoulder.

"You sure that's new?"

"It looks new. It looks like someone's tried to force it."

"Well, it could be it's the first time you've noticed it. Could be that the guy before you, whatshisname? Father O'Neil? Maybe he forgot his keys and tried to force the door."

Tanner was a big man, about the same height as Devlin, and solid with it. His hands were tanned and scaly from hard, outdoor labor and his face was badly pitted from what Devlin guessed might have been a bad case of teenage acne. His nose was pitted too, and bulbous from hard drinking. The truth was Devlin didn't know much about Tanner because, having taken over the role of sexton a few days ago, he was even more of a newcomer than Devlin. Devlin found it reassuring that, unlike everyone else in Avery, Tanner didn't treat Devlin as an outsider. The only thing Devlin did know about Tanner was that he had worked as a park ranger in Connecticut.

"Or I guess it could be the kids that come up here at night," Tanner continued. "I know the guy before me had trouble with them drinking and getting high in the graveyard."

"Yeah. That could be it."

"I'll keep an eye out, Father."

"Thanks."

"What's the day got in store for you?"

"A meeting with the Bishop." Devlin checked his watch. "Right now, in fact. Then I have a routine with the finance person."

"Sounds exciting."

"You?"

"I gotta drain to clear."

"Oh, right. I smelled that."

Tanner shrugged. "The place is just a patch-up job. Knew it as soon as I arrived. She needs proper renovation but all she gets is patched-up."

"Have a good day."

"You too, Father. God bless."

"God bless."

Devlin didn't have long before the meeting with the Bishop. He managed to splash some cold water on his face and then dumped some papers he'd been carrying around on the study desk. He rarely used the study; it was dusty, dark, and musty. An oil painting of a much younger Father O'Neil hung on the wall and was pretty much the only item O'Neil had left behind.

O'Neil had taken the contents of the desk drawers and cabinets with him. He'd packed up old records and paperwork, and got them couriered over to his sister's where he was convalescing. It was as if he were terrified Devlin might take over his territory, so he'd decided to take as much of it with him as he could.

Devlin opened one of the bottom desk drawers to throw in his papers. As he did a small round object, an old chestnut, dropped to the front. He picked it up and rolled it around between his thumb and finger. Tiny words had been painstakingly inscribed in the brown surface of the chestnut by what might have been a pin. Devlin brought the chestnut up close to his eye and, squinting hard, made out the Latin words *'ambo te ignosce me.'*

"I love you, forgive me," he muttered to himself then dropped the chestnut in his pocket and left the rectory.

Devlin walked around the perimeter of the church, past the front entrance, and through a gate that opened into a small courtyard on the east side of the church. The wind came and went in hard blasts with sprinkles of cold rain.

In the center of the courtyard was an old, lime-washed clapboard building in desperate need of care and attention. Another patch-up job. It was the church hall, where a good deal of church business was held.

Devlin opened the door and was greeted with a rush of mildewed air. Three men and a woman were sitting in a semi-circle of chairs, waiting. Under the creaking rafters and suffering the cold air was Bishop Molina. Seated next to him were two other men Devlin didn't recognize. On the other end of the semi-circle, visibly cowed by the presence of senior clergy, was Susan Hennessy, the finance officer, who gave her services free of charge. She had an iPad in a flowery case on her lap and a bulging leather handbag by her feet.

Bishop Molina was a man of unusually large proportions; his clerical suit had been cut generously to safely cover his heavily overweight frame. His pectoral cross was tucked into his shirt pocket and the gold chain lay across his great chest. He had a walking stick planted between his two ample legs.

Molina, Devlin, and Susan Hennessy exchanged hellos and then Molina extended a puffy hand toward the two men next two him.

"This is The Very Reverend Father Deeney, a priest for St. Mary's in Waltham, and The Very Reverend Father Lopez who ministers at three of our churches in Massachusetts. Both Father Deeney and Father Lopez are on the Archdiocese Board and do great work. Father Deeney also oversees religious education in the diocese. We were on our way to a board meeting in Boston and they have kindly accommodated this little stop off. I asked Mrs. Hennessy to attend as finance officer."

Devlin pulled a chair from a stack that had been pushed up against the wall and sat in front of the semi-circle.

"Father Deeney, Father Lopez, good to meet you."

There followed a silence while Devlin waited to hear why he'd received this small but grand delegation. The silence grew uncomfortable before Bishop Molina finally spoke. Leaning forward in his creaking chair he pressed down on his walking stick and stared solemnly at Devlin.

"Why, Father Devlin?"

"Why what?"

"Why are you here?"

"I was asked as a favor by a friend, Cardinal Hermes, to step in while Father O'Neil was convalescing."

"Yes, that bit I understand. It was made very clear to me by the Cardinal's office that my opinion about your temporary appointment would not be taken into account. But my question is more about you, Father. About what kind of priest you are. About why you've decided, after two years without a post, to come out here to Avery."

Both Susan Hennessy and Father Lopez, a young, officious-looking man, twitched in their seats. Father Deeney on the other hand looked completely unperturbed by the confrontation Bishop Molina was determined to create. If anything, he was watching with genuine interest.

"I mean," continued Molina, "what were you doing all that time?"

"I took a sabbatical. There were personal issues I thought I had found a kind of peace with. I was wrong."

"And now you have found a peace?"

"I've realized peace might not be my road. You could say, I've found a peace in not expecting I should be at peace."

"I'm not sure I'd want a priest serving in my Archdiocese who was at war with himself."

"With respect, Bishop Molina, that's not what I said."

Molina pushed the handle of his stick back and forth and let his gaze rest on the floor for a moment. "Why return now? Why do you need to serve a congregation now, but you couldn't two years ago?"

"Because I'm a better man than I was two years ago. A better priest."

Molina looked over at the two men beside him and then back at Devlin. "I'm going to be honest with you, Father Devlin. I have reservations about your character. Cardinal

Hermes, who has had a surprisingly fast rise to the top, doesn't share those reservations, but then he isn't a Bishop here. I don't trust priests who suddenly up and go, deserting their post and disappearing for years on end. I don't trust that kind of person's character. I don't even understand such a person."

"I do," said Father Deeney.

Surprised by the interjection, Molina turned to Deeney who was leaning forward in his seat. Unlike the younger Father Lopez he looked like he'd led a life and had some miles on the clock. His receding hair was fine, sandy, and long. His skin was deep-tanned but not from sunbathing; it was more like the deep-down tan of a ranch hand. His fingers were long and his knuckles stuck out like knots on a rope. His eyes were green and direct.

"I did a similar thing," Deeney continued. "For ten years I was on the road. Attached to no particular church. Going from place to place ministering. A street priest. Then I found a place I wanted to stay. Felt like I was being called to. So, I think I might understand a man like Father Devlin."

"I'm not sure at all that you're cut from the same cloth as Father Devlin, Father Deeney," said Molina. "However," — he turned to Devlin ruefully — "here you are. Having spent so long away from a congregation Father Devlin, you will have to prove your competence. I will be keeping an extremely close eye on you. I asked Mrs. Hennessy along because I wanted to make clear the limits of your appointment. As far as any long-term projects or significant financial decisions are concerned, they must go through the board. The financial arrangements and policies Father O'Neill put in place are to be followed, and any deviation felt necessary must also go through the board. Is that clear Mrs. Hennessy?"

Susan Hennessy nodded earnestly. Molina glanced at the

clock on the wall and then, with some difficulty, he stood. The others stood with him.

"I need to leave. My next appointment is in Boston."

"Thank you for dropping by, Your Grace," said Devlin.

"You'll see me again soon, Father Devlin."

Molina shuffled out accompanied by Father Lopez. Father Deeney stayed behind and approached Devlin, extending a hand.

"I'm very glad to have met you, Father Devlin."

Deeney's eyes, green and honest, fixed on Devlin's with surprising intensity and for a split second, Devlin felt as if those strange eyes were like a spotlight on his soul.

"I wouldn't worry about The Bishop," said Deeney. "He's not like you and me. For him religion is... Well, just religion. For men like you and I, it's the torment and the salvation, the beginning, and the end. He wouldn't understand you. But I think I do, or could. I think we might even be kindred spirits."

Not waiting for a reply, Deeney shook Devlin's hand again firmly and left, hurrying after the Bishop and Father Lopez, leaving Devlin a little bewildered.

Only he and Susan Hennessy, who had returned to her seat, remained.

"I thought we might go through outstanding business," said Susan, swiping across her iPad.

"Is there any, Susan? I mean, you heard the Bishop. I'm really only here to keep Father O'Neil's seat warm."

"Oh yes, there are things that you should at least know about."

Devlin sat in the chair nearest her. Susan tucked her hair behind her ears and swiped again at the tablet in her lap.

Susan Hennessy was a thorough, devout woman, slight and slim in stature. Though in her late fifties something of her youth remained. Her skin was taut and clear, and only a hint of gray troubled her shoulder-length blonde hair. She and her husband, the local police detective, were committed Catholics and very active in church fundraising activities. There was something about Susan Hennessy though that made Devlin uneasy. He felt she disapproved of him, in a similar way that the Bishop did. He suspected it was because she didn't think he was serious enough, dedicated enough. But most of all, he suspected it was because he wasn't Father O'Neil.

"First thing is just an FYI," said Susan. "We got a request from a teacher at Avery High who asked if she could do a project with her students up here. Going through the gravestones and cataloging the names, looking into the local family trees and history. Father O'Neil said no to it. He was adamant he didn't want kids crawling all over the place. Said it was a health and safety issue. Anyway, this morning she emailed to ask again, and I referred her to Father O'Neil's first answer."

"Okay."

"Then the main things to know are that Father O'Neil agreed to hire the new sexton, Mr. Tanner, on a temporary basis only. To see how he works out."

"Right."

"And, until he returns, Father O'Neil has forbidden undertaking any capital projects beyond necessary repair. That's really the headline."

"No work on the buildings? Have you seen the state of the place? The whole site needs serious investment."

"Father O'Neil was very clear that any major renovation would need to wait till he was back."

"Susan, look around you. Look at this place."

Susan glanced up at the cavernous, moldy old barn that served as the church hall.

"And there are the ruins of the old church in the field

behind," Devlin continued. "It's overgrown and in a dangerous state. Something needs to be done about it."

"We've contacted a contractor to come and secure the site. To properly fence it off."

"When's that happening?"

"Oh, soon, probably. They said they could do it in the new year. But Father O'Neil wouldn't want any long work undertaken in his absence. He's just very protective of his church."

Devlin sighed and nodded. "I understand that. And I know Father O'Neil is getting the best treatment there is and he'll be back here in a matter of months, by spring latest. But he may also need longer to recuperate. These things aren't always predictable. What I mean is, the church's renovation may not wait on Father O'Neil's renovations."

Susan didn't quote roll her eyes, but that disapproval Devlin had sensed seemed to rise a few degrees.

"Well, there's really no money to finance anything significant. And if you want to find more money to tackle the longer-term repairs, you'll need to go talk to Father O'Neil, and then that'd need the Bishop to agree. Or you could talk to Cardinal Hermes... I mean, he seems to think a lot of you."

From outside the gusts of wind had died down and voices, shouting, and laughing could be heard.

"Maybe I will." Devlin tapped his leg impatiently. "Anything else?"

Susan looked down the list in front of her one more time. "No. Those are the things I thought I should let you know about."

More voices and laughter came from the courtyard, causing Susan to look out the window. Outside was a group of kids huddled in a crowd with backpacks and clipboards.

"Who...? Who are the kids outside?" asked Susan.

"Oh, they're from Avery High. The teacher caught me on the

phone this morning. Asked me about the graveyard project you just mentioned. She's quite insistent. And I said yes."

"But... But Father O'Neil was absolutely clear —"

"Come on, Susan. It's a great idea."

"Father O'Neil will not be happy at all."

"Blame it on me, Susan. Just blame it all on me." Devlin stood and smiled. "Let's go outside and meet them."

Devlin and Susan stepped out into the courtyard. There were about a dozen kids, grades eight and nine, milling around in high spirits and big winter coats.

The wind had calmed down now, though dark clouds still scudded fast across the sky, causing the sharp winter light to come and go, producing a curious effect. Shadows appeared and vanished so fast they seemed to alter the shape and colors of the yard in an almost unreal, dreamlike way.

In the middle of the group of kids, hushing them and handing out worksheets, was a woman in her thirties wearing a light wool coat, a beanie, and a scarf. She waved at Devlin and walked over.

"Hi, Father. Thanks so much for letting us do this project."

"No problem at all, Miss Wilson. I think it's a great idea."

"Susan, this is Sarah Wilson, a teacher at Avery High. I believe you've exchanged emails."

Sarah turned to Susan who, having said no to the project, was pink with embarrassment. Sarah didn't seem to harbor any ill will.

"Hi, Mrs. Hennessy," she said through a warm smile. "I didn't say in my emails, but I know your husband, Detective Hennessy. Ted comes every year to give a talk to my grade eights. He does such a great job."

"Thank you." She glanced down at her watch. "I should go. I have to take my mother to a hospital appointment."

Susan didn't wait for goodbyes but scooted past the students, keeping her distance.

Sarah watched Susan leave and turned back to Devlin. "We'll be on best behavior, Father. I've told the kids they are to be respectful here at all times. Just tell me all the ground rules and we'll stick to them to the letter."

"Ground rules? I don't have any ground rules. I'm happy to have them here bringing some life and energy to the place."

"Oh, okay. Great. Say, you're quite a change from Father O'Neil."

"Well, you've heard the phrase 'broad church.' You have free run of the place and I look forward to the results of the project."

"Me too. I think it's a great thing for the church and the town."

"I'll let you all get on... Oh, wait, there is one thing I should say, there are the ruins of the old church in the field behind. They'll be out of bounds to the kids I'm afraid. It's overrun and falling to pieces, and just not safe."

"Oh, sure. Of course. Although that might be a project I'd be interested in myself. I'm a bit of an amateur historian. Teaching history and all. And I'm head of the Avery History Society. And the Avery Conservation Society. Truth is, I have a finger in most of the pies in terms of local activities. I'm a big 'take-parter.' Is that a word? It should be. What do you think?"

"Well, that's certainly possible, Miss Wilson."

"Sarah, it's Sarah. Let's grab a coffee sometime soon? I'd love to talk that through."

"Let's do that."

"Sooner the better for me. We could pencil in a day later in the week?"

Devlin smiled.

"What? What's so funny?"

"I think I understand the urgency. You want to get this going before Father O'Neil comes back."

"Can you blame me?"

"No. No, I can't."

"I mean, he's a real party pooper. I don't even think I've ever seen him smile."

"He's not a well man."

"Yeah. Sorry. Of course. I forgot. I guess he hasn't got much to smile about."

"No. But he'll be back. God willing."

The kids were getting restless and Sarah called out to them to settle down.

"I should get back to the students."

"I'll leave you to it."

"Thanks again, Father. I appreciate this so much." Sarah threw out a hand and Devlin shook it.

"No problem..."

The light was playing about the yard again, moving shadow and color. As the winter sun danced and faded behind the clouds it had the strangest effect on Devlin. The shadows and light passing over Sarah's face gave the fleeting impression that her features were shifting, almost as if her face was transforming. Then the sun came out from behind the cloud and the illusion vanished.

"Are you okay, Father?"

The noise of the children had momentarily faded away but now returned, and Devlin began to wonder if he'd had enough sleep.

"Yes. Yes. I'm fine. Let's get that coffee. Text or call me with times you're free."

4

The change in Father O'Neil was dramatic. The treatment intended to cure him had also ravaged him. Dark rings circled his hollow eyes. He had lost twenty, maybe even thirty pounds since Devlin had last seen him, and he'd been a slight man to begin with. He sat in an armchair swaddled in a thick woolen cardigan, imprisoned in a constant pain dulled by controlled medication. His pale features were softened by the low glow of a table lamp.

O'Neil was staying with his sister Patricia in Manchester-by-the-Sea. She was providing the care he needed while he convalesced and got through the grueling treatment. She made tea for the two men when Devlin arrived and, as Devlin and O'Neil talked, she could be heard about the house, busy clearing things away in other rooms.

The conversation was halting and peppered with silences.

"How long will the course of chemotherapy be?" asked Devlin.

"Another month. It's exhausting. A terrible business. But I have my faith. I have my faith."

"I'm praying for your good health and recovery."

"Yes, prayer and chemo, that's what I call complimentary medicine." O'Neil uttered a wry laugh which turned into a coughing fit. He reached for a tissue from the box on the table next to him and muffled his mouth until the attack had passed. Then he dabbed his lips dry.

"But I don't think you came here to talk to me about my disease, did you, Father Devlin?"

"I always intended to come by after the operation. But, you're right, I also have some church business to discuss with you. I met with the Bishop this morning."

"Oh, how did it go?"

Devlin thought he detected a sparkle in O'Neil's tired eyes.

"I think you have a good idea how it went."

"Maybe. Maybe not."

"I think you know that the Bishop is not my greatest fan."

"Oh, I wouldn't take it personally."

"I don't."

"You're a smart man, Father. You'll have worked out for yourself that the Bishop probably feels undermined by Cardinal Hermes insisting on you being installed as my replacement."

"I also met with Susan to go through church business. It quickly became clear that I don't have much of a remit at Holy Cross. That, at your insistence, I am not allowed to undertake any short, medium, or long-term planning or projects."

"You are only my temporary replacement."

"I think the restrictions are too severe. They don't allow me the freedom to do the job I'm being asked to do. They go against the best interests of the church."

"That is not my view."

"Could you expand on your view?"

O'Neil sighed. "There's nothing to expand upon. I don't know what it is you want me to say."

"The truth. Just the truth."

O'Neil smiled. "The truth? Well, as it happens that's very straightforward. The truth is, I don't trust you. But that should be obvious to a fool. After all, what sort of priest disappears from his church for two years? You deserted your congregation, the church you swore to serve. Your behavior was disgraceful. You are only at Holy Cross because you have a powerful friend who overruled both mine and the Bishop's wishes. That is the truth. But even though I could not prevent your appointment, I can lay down the terms of your tenure. I will make sure that you will only be priest at Holy Cross in the narrowest of meanings. There to keep it running in the strictest sense. Even though I don't think you're suitable to minister at Holy Cross, I can limit the damage you do. And, mark my words, I will see off this wretched disease and I will come back to Holy Cross." With some effort, Father O'Neil leaned forward in his chair. "And I will see you off too."

"I don't doubt it. Yet prayer alone won't keep the building from falling apart. And, if while you're away something does go badly wrong, what am I to do?"

"If that happens it will be a matter for myself and the Bishop to handle. Now, I'm tired. I need to rest. You will excuse me if I don't see you to the door."

Devlin stood. He paused for a moment and looked down at Father O'Neil with a directness that made O'Neil uncomfortable.

"We are very different kinds of priests you and I... Different kinds of men. We don't get along. Probably never will. However, I only wish you the best, Father O'Neil. I am praying for your speedy recovery and my prayers are genuine."

Avoiding eye contact, O'Neil mumbled a thanks.

Devlin reached the doorway, then stopped and turned. "There was something else I wanted to ask you about."

"What?"

"I think someone's been trying to break into the rectory."

O'Neil's frail form was suddenly jolted by this news. "What?"

"This morning. I noticed the front door to the rectory had been damaged. It looked like someone had tried to force the door."

"Did you report it to the police?"

"Yes. I did."

"You should tell the sexton to keep an eye out."

"I did that too."

Devlin frowned and O'Neil saw something was troubling him. "What? What is it?"

"Have you ever had that happen before? Someone try and break in?"

"No. Never!" O'Neil's reply was emphatic.

"Okay. I'll keep an eye out too. The sexton thinks it's kids, and he's probably right."

Devlin left and O'Neil watched the headlights of his car wash across the windows and swing out into the road. He felt for his cross under his cardigan, clutched it, and prayed to himself in soft, mournful tones.

5

It was the middle of nowhere. A dirt track through half a dozen fields that ended in a clearing bounded by a strip of woodland. Somewhere beyond the woodland, he could hear the sound of a fast running river, also beyond that traffic. He double-checked the What-Three-Words app he'd been told to download. It looked like he was in the right place, even if the right place was miles from anywhere. He jumped out of his van and had a look around. Nothing. Nobody anywhere. The truth was it was creepy out here. This was the first time his boss had done business this far east, so the whole deal was new. The Driscoll family were new business partners and this was new procedure. Even by the usual standards, this was weird.

He lit a cigarette and checked his cell. He'd give it ten minutes then call. His boss had a temper and it was three in the morning so he only wanted to call in if it was serious.

He took a drag on his smoke, scanned the dark edges of the clearing, and saw a flashlight twinkle in the bushes. The light was bobbing up and down as if it were being held by someone walking. Sure enough, the light got closer and the person holding it became clearer.

"Hey," shouted the figure with the flashlight.

"Hey," he shouted back.

"You found the place."

"Yeah. Followed the app just like you said. This is really the drop-off?"

"Yeah. This is it." The guy with the flashlight was up close now. He was tall and lean with a shock of red hair slicked back. "Name's Callum Driscoll. Tony's son. Unload the delivery."

"What? Here?"

"Yeah. Here."

"But we're in the middle of nowhere. There ain't a building or road for miles around."

"You just let me worry about that. Unload the truck and drive off. It's not complicated."

He threw his cigarette on the ground and put his hands up. "Okay. If that's what you want."

Then he unloaded the van while Callum Driscoll watched. It took ten minutes to stack all the cargo on the grass. Callum Driscoll did a random check, ripping open half a dozen of the packages to check the contents. Then he stood back and nodded.

"You're all good," said Driscoll. "We'll handle it from here."

"Okay, boss. Whatever you say." He got back in his van, started the engine, and, as he drove back the way he came, he watched Driscoll in his mirror standing still in the dark.

"What a crazy setup. Wait till I tell the boys about this one," he mumbled as he followed the narrow dirt track back toward the sound of the freeway.

6

The doorbell chimed at the same moment the microwave pinged. Sarah Wilson left her Thai Green curry steaming in its plastic tray and plodded in her slippers across the fake wood flooring to the door.

"This better not be another delivery for next door," she muttered to herself. "Why aren't they ever in?"

She peered through the peephole and immediately wished it had been a parcel for the neighbors. Then she opened the door, her heart thudding.

"Sarah."

"Hi, Tom."

It was the first time they'd been face to face since the big night three weeks ago. The big breakup. She'd ignored his calls and insisted on communicating by text only.

"How did you get my address?"

"You ordered a new TV on our joint account. I got emailed a receipt and the address it was going to."

She silently cursed her stupidity. "Right."

"Can I come in? For five minutes, that's all. We gotta talk

sometime. Even if it's just to start sorting out all the practical stuff."

Sarah stepped away from the door and indicated with a nod that Tom could enter. Tom took a look around the place.

"It's kind of an out-of-the-way place. Took a while to find it."

"I didn't ask you to come, Tom."

"Yeah. No... Sure. It's not very homely."

Sarah looked around the one-bed rental, at the white walls, the bare floors, the lonely couch, the new TV, and the minimal kitchenette. The smell of a microwave meal hanging in the air topped the whole thing off. Then she thought of the cozy three bed she'd had with Tom. Still had with Tom. And why she could no longer live there.

"Did you just come here to critique the interior decor?"

Tom walked over to the couch and sat on one end of it, leaving space for Sarah. Sarah dragged a chair over instead.

"I'm not radioactive," said Tom.

Sarah couldn't think of a smart reply so she said nothing. She watched him play with his Apple Watch strap and squirm. Inside she was squirming too. She still found him attractive, still loved him. He was tall and slim with untidy blonde hair, and looked good in his pea-coat and cords that fitted snugly around his long legs. His cheeks were a little red from the cold and his brown eyes shone. There were, no doubt, other women who would do things differently to Sarah and give into those feelings. It turned out she was not those other women.

"How are things?" asked Tom.

"Fine. School's fine... Fine. You?"

"Ah, I'm thinking I should have never taken the secondment at the Department of Education. It's really dry stuff. I'll be glad to get back to teaching."

"You wanted to get some experience in the policy side, so that's good."

"Yeah, that's good."

"Have you put the place on the market yet?"

"I have someone coming round tomorrow. They say it can be on their website and Zillow by the end of the week. But..."

"But what?"

"I don't want to sell."

"How else are you going to pay me back my equity?"

"Jeez... Come on, Sarah..."

"'Come on Sarah' what?"

"Do you have to be so hard-assed about this?"

"I'm living in an apartment that's smaller than some people's bathrooms and I'm paying rent and a mortgage. I need our apartment sold."

He rubbed his mop of hair and sighed. Then he dabbed his eye with the back of his hand.

"I didn't come here to talk about selling the goddamn apartment. I came here to beg you to come back. Please." Despite the dabbing, his eyes were wet with tears. "Please, Sarah. Come back. I'm so sorry."

Sarah felt the pull of her former life. The pull of her handsome fiancé and spacious split-level apartment furnished with pieces they had hunted for together on Saturdays in Cambridge Antique Market. The pull of a wedding date and the family she was destined to have.

"How many times?" asked Sarah.

"What?"

"How many times?"

"We've been through all of this..."

"First, you don't get to tell me when you think we've been through this. Second, you've never told me how many times."

"Twice. It was twice."

She'd known it was more than once. And with a mutual friend. Although the mutual friend — whose name she couldn't bring herself to say — had always been more Tom's friend than hers.

"You know, Tom, the reason I left is not just because you slept with someone else. It was because I knew something had happened and you lied to me. And you kept lying to me, making me feel like I was some wretched, needy, insecure girlfriend. You were so... righteous about it. So insistent that I was the crazy one. And I believed you. Until I found out for myself. Because you were never going to tell me the truth. You slept with someone else. Twice. And you made it seem like I was making it all up, like I was to blame, and the worst thing of all is, I still feel like that."

Tom was looking directly at Sarah, his face red with heartbreak and shame. "I know perfectly well what I did. It was all my fault. I hate myself for it. And I am so, so sorry."

"I know you're sorry. I wish that was enough. It's the way you acted afterward, Tom. The way you made me feel like I was someone I'm not. And never will be. I think you enjoyed how it made me feel."

"I never enjoyed how it made you feel. It tore me apart... All of it... And I absolutely understand how my behavior made you feel and why it was completely unacceptable."

"You don't, Tom."

"What do you mean, I don't? You can't tell me what I do and don't understand."

"Because you wouldn't be here. If you really understood then I don't think you'd even be here."

Tom wanted to say something. But he realized that everything he wanted to say would make him look smaller or foolish, or both. The reality was, only *he* wanted to talk anymore. Sarah just wanted him to leave.

He walked to the door, stopping halfway to deliver one more line. "You know, Sarah, the one thing you lack, you've always lacked, is the capacity to forgive. In a way, I'm glad I at least found that out now."

And then he was gone.

WHAT A JERK. He'd done it again. His special trick. At the end of an argument, no matter how badly he'd behaved, somehow he'd manage to hang something on her.

Sarah opened the microwave and peered in at the tray of congealed matter. She slid out the still-warm container and dropped it into the trash. Then she ordered a pizza and opened a bottle of cheap red wine. In quick succession, she downed two large glasses on an empty stomach and was well on her way back to being tipsy.

Cross-legged on the couch, munching on a slice of margarita, she caught her reflection on the TV screen.

SHE LOOKED at the outline of her face and remembered the visit to the medium. She put her glass down, crawled on all fours up to the screen, and inspected her features in the black glass. There was nothing there. No other person trying to get out. And her heart sank because that meant she really was on her own. A familiar feeling washed over her, a feeling she'd had all her life, a feeling of not being in the right place, of not fitting in. She wondered if everyone felt the same, and if they felt it with the same intensity as she did.

She lay out on the couch and let the wine do its work. Woozy and warm, she drifted off listening to the rain on the window and fell into a deep dream.

In her dream, she was a young girl again. A boy she had never met — but had no doubt she knew — walked up to her and, one after the other, pulled out both of his eyes.

"Try them," he said with red holes in his head.

"But they're not mine."

"Try them," he said again with red tears rolling down his cheeks. "They fit just right."

So, she held them up to her eyes and the two round, wet balls jumped into her head. The boy was correct. They fitted just right.

"Now you can see what I see. Look up."

Sarah looked up and saw that above her were the tops of trees and a night sky. Stars raced across the sky and night turned into day then back into night again. The switch from day to night carried on, becoming faster and faster until the sky blinked dark and light and the seasonal foliage on the trees came and went at terrific speed. Then it all suddenly stopped. It was back to night, and in the dark sky Sarah saw something that looked like a yellow bundle of seven snakes.

"What does it mean?" Sarah asked the boy. But the boy wasn't there anymore. In his place was a man in a robe whose face was covered by a hood. The man in the robe rushed toward her and Sarah felt warm liquid explode over her front.

She woke to find wine everywhere, including her jumper and pants and the couch cushions.

"Damn."

The clock on Sarah's iPhone said 3am. She'd woken with a headache, sore eyes, and red wine all over the place.

Feeling a bit sick, she cleared up the mess with a tea towel, got out of her clothes, threw them in the washing machine, and got into her pajamas.

In bed, she felt scared and vulnerable. Scared of the man in the robe. That he might be lurking in the dark corners of the apartment. She kept all the lights on and went to sleep with the radio on and her phone by her pillow.

7

"I don't know. It looks so dark."

"Yeah. That's kind of the point, dumbass."

The nearest lights, the yellow ground lights that lit up the walls of Holy Cross Church, were a couple of hundred yards away. But back here, by the high chain-link fence that cordoned off the old Holy Cross Church ruins, it was scarily dark.

The braver of the two boys, a kid with a shaved head and a baggy hoodie, had scaled the fence and was straddling the top. The other boy, slighter and smaller with his hoodie up and his long hair covering most of his face, looked up in awe.

"What can you see?" From the ground, he could only see a few yards past the fence into thick, overgrown woodland.

The boy on the top of the fence squinted through the gaps in the tree tops. "Not much. Come on, Ash. Climb the fence." He swung his leg over and, with a nimbleness Ash could only admire, he slipped down to the ground on the other side.

Reluctantly Ash scaled the fence and, making far heavier work of it, tipped over the top and clumsily descended the other side, joining his friend. He took a look around.

"Kai, this is scary."

"Yeah. I wanna see what the old church is like. If it's as spooky as they say it is." Kai pulled a ready-rolled joint out of his hoodie pocket, lit it up, and took a hit.

He exhaled a mixture of smoke and condensed breath then passed the joint to Ash, who took a nip, coughed, and handed it back to Kai. "Let's go take a look-see."

Kai took off and Ash scrambled after him, moving awkwardly between the close standing trees, his feet navigating the thick brush and bits of trash that had been dumped by other trespassers. Moon and starlight filtered down through the tree-tops, lending enough pale light to see. It felt to Ash as if a murdering lunatic lay in wait behind every tree. And if they did run into someone, what then? What were the chances that anyone hanging out here, in the middle of a deserted bit of land in the small hours of the night, would have good intentions? They would probably have the worst of intentions and every license to carry those intentions out. Panic filled Ash, but he was too far in to start back by himself. Better he stuck with Kai who was bigger, stronger, and braver.

"Hey...!" Kai's voice was high and hoarse. He was just a few yards ahead of Ash. "I see it. Wow..."

Kai's pace had slowed as he came out into a clearing. After a few moments, Ash joined him.

In front of the boys, standing in a low mist that made it appear half-dreamed and half-real, they saw the crumbing remains of an old granite church. It was simple and plain in design, rectangular, and with a bell tower at the far end. The windows had long since gone and parts of the roof had fallen in. The window arches and porches were scorched black from a fire. Ivy and weeds had forced their way through gaps in the stones and overrun the structure.

The building seemed to stare down at the two boys with

charred eyes, affronted at its uninvited visitors and warning them to leave.

The boys shared a few more hits on the joint then Kai flicked it away.

"I don't think it's safe, Kai."

"I know it's not safe."

"Do you think there are bats?"

"Yeah, probably. This is like the Four Seasons for bats. But they'll be asleep."

"Bats sleep during the day, dumbass."

"They'll be asleep 'cos they're hibernating, dumbass."

"It must be used for something. Marshall Beck said he came down here and saw trucks come around the back. In the middle of the night."

"Marshall Beck's full of crap. Let's go inside."

Again Ash considered his options. Yet again they boiled down to being alone in the middle of nowhere in the middle of the night or following his friend into the unknown. He followed Kai into the ruins.

If the outside of the church had been forbidding, the inside was downright hostile. A little moonlight spilled in, through the spaces where windows had once been and through the gaps in the roof. There was nowhere near enough light to disperse the darkness that concealed most of the interior.

"Awesome," said Kai.

"What now?"

"Let's have another smoke."

Ash's head was already soft and cloudy but they both smoked another ready-rolled and began to feel their way around the church using the flashlights on their cells. There was no furniture left, just mounds of trash on the floor and graffiti left by generations of other trespassers.

Despite the effects of the grass Ash began to feel braver. He roamed a little farther away from Kai toward the chancel and found steps that led up to the apse. Cautiously, and as if in slow motion, Ash climbed the four steps onto the stone floor where once the altar would have been. He looked up, raising his cell phone flashlight, peering into the blackness to see if there was still a cross on display. He was relieved to see that too had gone. He stepped forward to explore the recesses of the apse.

Kai was up at the other end and retching from the sour stink of urine when he heard the scream. It was loud and wild and terrified.

"Ash...! Ash...?" He heard his voice echo back, but no reply.

He headed back along the nave, wading through the filth, moving like an astronaut on the moon through the dark, and the broken glass and garbage. He followed the sound of Ash's whimpers, and when he got to the apse he saw what Ash had failed to see; a square opening in the floor. He waved his light at the opening and called down.

"Ash...? Ash...? You okay?"

For a terrifying couple of seconds there was no reply.

"Yeah... I think so..." said Ash, his voice weak and thin.

"What's down there?"

"More trash. Lot's more trash."

Kai saw steps leading down into the chamber, which he cautiously descended, and found his friend standing in more garbage. They pointed their cell lights at each other.

"Sure you're okay?" asked Kai again.

"Sure," replied Ash who had started brushing himself down. "Just covered in crap."

"It smells bad down here."

There was a heavy odor of earth, piss, and dampness. Kai swung his cell light over the profanity-daubed walls and then behind Ash.

"Hey, there's another room."

Ash looked behind him. "Oh yeah."

The two boys moved forward into a second chamber which was accessed through an archway. In this second part, the stone floor stopped and instead became hard, compacted earth.

Ash swung his cell up to the ceiling.

"What's that?"

Above the two boys was a large drawing of what looked like a tree or a bundle of wheat.

"I think we should go," said Ash. "We've been here long enough, haven't we?"

Kai wasn't listening. His cell light was pointed into the corner of the room where the earth had been scratched away. He moved closer to inspect the disturbed earth. At first, he thought he was looking at more random trash, but it slowly dawned on him that the piece of trash looked an awful lot like the side of a skull. He felt cold fear and a deranged scream rising inside of him. But the scream died in his throat because of the growl that was coming from the other side of the chamber.

The two boys froze. Out of the unknown came two yellow eyes and a flash of sharp, long, dirty teeth. There was a brief silence, a fierce bark, and the sound of trickling. Ash realized that urine was pooling around the bottom of his sneaker. A wolf, large and wild, had come entirely out of the shadows, baring its teeth, its growl rising to a crescendo. When the bark came it leaped up and toward Kai, jaw open, aiming for the throat. Then the whole chamber lit up in a flash of white and filled with a boom that sounded like the end of the world.

The dust cleared and a smell of gunpowder filled the crypt.

"You boys shouldn't be here."

The boys heard a rough, low voice but didn't take the words in. Their ears were ringing and bright lights swam in front of their eyes. On the floor lay the wolf, the side of its face an obliterated, bloody mess.

"Hey."

The boys looked around and saw the outline of a tall, mean-looking old guy in the doorway. Along with a shotgun, he was holding a flashlight. He moved closer, close enough so they could see his face, all pitted and pink.

"I'm the sexton here," he said. "I look after the grounds. You boys are trespassing."

"But... But..." stammered Kai. "The wolf."

"Coy-wolf. We don't have wolves round here. Not anymore." The sexton cocked his head and looked at the slain animal. "Though he is a big sonofabitch. Come on, let's go."

"Wait," said Ash. "There's something else..."

He pointed at the disturbed earth in the corner. "Bones..."

The sexton swung his flashlight into the corner. Encased in the dirt floor he spotted the yellow and brown shape of a skull.

8

Unable to sleep, Devlin had gotten up and thrown on a t-shirt, pants, boots, and an overcoat, then slipped out into the night to smoke. He'd been staring at the night sky, halfway through his cigar, when he had heard a distant boom like a shotgun going off. The sound had come from the old church, so Devlin headed in that direction. Finding the gate unlocked, he went to investigate.

On the other side of the thick strip of forest, in front of the old church, he found the two boys looking sorry for themselves. Hoyt Tanner stood holding his shotgun across his body.

"What happened?"

Tanner took Devlin aside.

"I heard voices in the old church so I took my shotgun and went looking. I found these kids trespassing, Father. Down in the crypt, below the apse. There was a coy-wolf down there. He was going for one of them so I let the mutt have it."

Devlin looked back at the kids. "Do you think they're the ones who tried to break into the rectory?"

"I already asked them that, but they denied it. Don't know if they were telling the truth but they seemed pretty convincing. There's something else though..."

"What?"

"There's a body down there. A skeleton. Looks human. Partially buried. Looks like animals have been digging it up. I guess it's a grave..."

"There are no graves in the crypt."

Devlin's firm and unequivocal reply took Tanner by surprise. "How do you know?"

"I had to look at the archives for a burial here just after I came to Holy Cross. We have a map of the plots in the old graveyard. There are none recorded in the crypt."

"You sure?"

"I'm sure there's no record of it. The only recorded burials were in the cemetery. Am I sure it's not a church grave that wasn't recorded? No." Devlin glanced over at the old church. "I'm going to take a look. You should call the police and keep the kids here."

Tanner called after Devlin but he was already heading toward the ruins.

Inside the old church, Devlin switched his cell flashlight on and found the opening in the floor of the apse. In the crypt below he located the corpse of the coy-wolf and, in the corner, the exposed skull. The right side of the skull was completely visible, and beneath it Devlin made out vertebrae and a right collar bone. There was nothing around the skull to indicate it had ever been an official grave.

Devlin knelt by the skull and studied its shape and size. He peered inside the jaw, opening it wider with his fingers and brushing out the dirt till he could see rows of teeth. His eyes traveled down to the neck vertebrae and the collar bone. Bending lower he inspected the area under the chin with particular care.

He stood and moved his flashlight over the floor and the dead coy-wolf with half a face left. Next he passed his light over the walls and up to the ceiling, where he discovered the painted symbol Ash and Kai had seen.

When Devlin emerged from the old church entrance two uniformed police were already in attendance, talking to Tanner and the two boys. Tanner indicated in Devlin's direction and one of the officers approached him.

"Hello, Father."

Devlin recognized the officer. He was Detective Sergeant Ted Hennessy, the husband of Susan Hennessy, the church's finance officer. He was short, with a mustache, and wore a flight jacket that exaggerated the extra weight he carried.

"Detective Hennessy. Thanks for coming out."

"No problem at all." He planted his hands on his holster, puffed his cheeks and exhaled condensed air. "The sexton over there says there's a body in the crypt."

"That's right."

"It'll be a burial then?"

"There's no record of any burial in the old church. Only in the cemetery."

"You're sure?"

"That's what the records say."

"It's possible it's just a regular burial that wasn't recorded though? Or over time the records were lost? After all, it's an old church. It shut down about seventy years ago. That would make sense to me."

"That's possible. But there are other things. Things about the body that don't make sense if it was a regular burial."

"Like what?"

"The way it's buried. It's not deep enough for an official burial for one thing. And..."

"And what?"

"Maybe it's best you just take a look."

Devlin led the way with the aid of Hennessy's flashlight, descending again into the dank rooms of the crypt and stopping by the archway to the second chamber.

"In the corner," Devlin said, pointing. Hennessy took a couple of steps further inside and ran his flashlight over the remains in the corner.

"The body is on its side," said Devlin.

"Could it have moved?"

"Maybe. If the ground shifted. Though there's nothing to suggest that's happened here. And it was a shallow grave. A few feet deep. Not deep enough for a religious burial. And there's something else too. I think whoever this was suffered a violent death."

"How can you tell that?"

"The hyoid bone is broken."

"The what?"

"It's the semi-circular bone underneath the chin."

Hennessy pointed his flashlight at the half-emerged skull and vertebrae. Then he stepped forward and crouched down by the skull. "What? That little thing? That could have broken anytime in the ground."

"I don't think so. It's a clean break, perimortem. If it was post-mortem the break would have been crumbly, and would have splintered not snapped."

Hennessy switched his flashlight over to Devlin. "Father, I don't mean to be rude, but this isn't your field of expertise."

"No. But I used to be a paramedic in the Air Force, pararescue. I'm not a pathologist but I do have training and experience. There's nothing about this body that looks like it was an official burial. I think whoever this was, they were strangled."

Hennessy sighed and scratched the side of his face. "You know, you're a lot different from Father O'Neil."

"Also, I don't think the body can have been here before the late sixties."

"How in the hell would you know that?"

"An educated guess. The teeth have white fillings. Not amalgam. White fillings started being used in the sixties. The last burial here was just after the Second World War. 1949. So that would point to it not being a burial."

"Well, I've never heard of that and it's pretty damn speculative."

Hennessy waved his flashlight around and saw the symbol on the ceiling.

"No idea what that is," said Devlin. "It looks like it could be a tree. Maybe the tree of life."

"Like Adam and Eve? The Garden of Eden?"

"Maybe."

Hennessy focused back on the skeleton. "Thing is, it's got to be at least a decade old for that amount of decomposition. If there's any possibility it's a homicide I have to call the Investigations Bureau in Worcester to come take a look." Hennessy sighed. "But the really puzzling thing is, Avery's a small and quiet town and I've been a cop for fifteen years... I've never heard of anyone going missing. Never. So, if this is what you say it is, then who the hell is it?"

9

From the moment the boy had escaped he'd had the strongest feeling that he was being followed. Or chased? A feeling that something dark and unnatural was tracking him, following his scent. A couple of weeks ago he wouldn't have believed such a crazy idea. Yet now, after what he'd seen, he could easily believe it.

He bedded down in the doorway of an office building with a sleeping bag he'd bought from a place called Tent City. It was the warmest and thickest they had but he was still cold. Since the incident with the guy from the pawn shop, he'd had real difficulty sleeping. His dreams were often a re-run of the moments leading up to him hitting the guy over the head with a brick, and then he'd wake up in a sweat.

The office porch was deep and wide enough that he couldn't be seen from the street. The sign on the building said it was an insurance company and the kid figured it kept pretty regular hours. There were no lights on and no security guard in the lobby. He set his cell phone alarm for six in the morning, early enough that he'd be back on the road before the building opened up.

The stone floor was cold and out on the street it was frosted over. He slipped the hood of the sleeping bag over his head and zipped it up. Then he curled his body tight, as if he were a cat wrapping around itself, and dropped off almost as soon as he closed his eyes.

When he next woke it was to the sound of a siren. He craned his neck and squinted at the big gold clock hanging in the lobby. It was 3am.

The siren came closer. He shivered, not wanting to have to get out of the bag. Not yet.

In the blurred dark, he saw a car slow to a crawl and approach along the curb. It was a cop car and the sirens had been turned off. He wasn't sure if they'd see him nestled in the porch, but he couldn't take the risk. He couldn't be caught by the cops. If he were caught he'd be sent back. Or sent to prison. So he braced himself, unzipped the bag, and slid out of it. It was so tired and he was so cold, cold right down to his marrow.

As the car came closer he edged out of the porch and, keeping low, he followed the wall of the building into a side yard which led into a parking lot. The lot had a couple of small roads leading out. He took one of the roads and came onto a deserted main street.

On this street so early in the morning, it was as quiet as the world ever got. No cars, no people; just him, the moon, and the stars. He walked down the street, his sleeping bag wrapped around him and his backpack hanging on his shoulders, looking for another place to bed down.

Yet, although the street was empty and there wasn't a cop car or any other car in sight, he still had the feeling he was being followed.

The boy scolded himself, playing out the role of a reasonable adult.

"Jamie," he said to himself, "there's no one there. You're just imagining things."

Still, the feeling got stronger.

He walked a block and stopped, looking back at the patches of ground frost glittering under a bright full moon. He spied a pharmacy across the street with a recessed door that looked like a promising place to bed down. He scooted across the road to take a closer look and decided it was acceptable. Desperate to crawl back into his sleeping bag, Jamie took one more look around and stopped dead. In among the shadows, up at the last intersection, he thought he could make out a figure. Was he imagining it? Was there someone standing there? He squinted hard. The more he looked, the more he thought he could see someone; a man in the middle of the road wearing a long robe with the cowl hood up shadowing his face.

No, thought Jamie. *It can't be. Not him.* How could he know that Jamie was here? He squinted at the black shape but still couldn't be sure of what he was seeing. Was it his sore eyes, shadows, and street lights playing tricks on him?

Jamie broke into a sprint immediately, powering down a road that led to a vast, windswept square. On the other side of the square were more office buildings, more of the anonymous blocks that made up the financial district. He stopped and looked back. In the distance he swore he could see the cloaked figure rushing down the street behind him, moving as if his feet weren't even touching the ground. Either he was losing his mind or... The other possibility was even worse.

"No. He can't have found me here."

At breakneck pace, Jamie took off again, his sleeping bag wound around his neck and body, his backpack knocking against his back. He wasn't much at anything but the one thing he was something at was running. With his long legs, he could run a hundred yards in twelve seconds. Anyone who wanted to catch him had their work cut out.

He flew across the square, through an intersection, and into another wide street bounded by gray-stone office buildings. He kept running, sprinting for another block until he began to feel the power drain from his legs and his stamina fade. Suddenly he heard a rush of air and a giant hiss.

A night bus had turned onto the street. Its turn signal was on and it was pulling over toward a bus stop.

Jamie borrowed all the energy his body would give him and took off like a rocket. He overtook the bus as it came to stop and waited for the doors to open. He took another look back along the street.

"You getting on or what?" asked the bus driver, now glaring down at the boy. Jamie jumped up the steps. He pulled a ten dollar bill from his pocket and thrust it toward the driver.

"Where are you going?"

"End of the line."

The driver pulled a face and counted out the change.

The door hissed shut. The bus started up. Jamie staggered down the empty carriage to the back seat. He stared out of the bus's rear window. The street was empty and he wondered if he was losing his mind.

They met on the outskirts of town. Susan Hennessy worked nearby and Devlin had time before Mass to make the short drive to the diner Susan had suggested.

Susan was sitting at a two-top by the corner beneath the specials chalkboard. She had her tablet in front of her and was peering down at it, scrolling nimbly with one finger. She wore a light brown silky blouse and had a yellow wool cardigan draped over her shoulders with the sleeves tied around her neck. There was a mug of coffee and a plate of crumbs in front of her. When she saw Devlin approach she offered a quick smile.

"Thank you for coming across town, Father."

"Not a problem."

There was a silence. Susan seemed to be perched forward in her chair, anxious to get to the meaty gossip, Devlin guessed, about the remains found beneath the old church. Before she could get her words out the waitress sidled up to take Devlin's order. Devlin stuck to a coffee. As soon as the waitress had filled his cup and left them alone, Susan Hennessy began talking at a clip about the events of the previous night.

"Ted told me what happened. At the old church."

"Yeah. Quite a thing."

"He says you think it wasn't an official burial."

"It's fair to say I'm yet to be convinced."

"But surely it makes sense it was a burial in the old church. Of course, none of us knew the priest back then. I'm pretty sure that any of the staff at the old Holy Cross or the diocese from that time aren't alive. But it's got to be a burial. Common sense would tell you it is."

Devlin wasn't sure how much Detective Ted Hennessy had told his wife, whether he'd told her that Devlin thought the body showed signs of strangulation. Whatever she knew it damn sure wasn't going to come from him.

"I know as little as you. I'm just gonna wait for the Bureau guys to do their work."

"In the meantime? What will happen in the meantime? Allowing speculation that it's a murder will be an excuse for all sorts of unsavory gossip to run wild about the town."

"I don't care what people gossip about. I asked to meet you, Susan, face to face, about the financial situation," said Devlin, leaning in.

"What about the financial situation?"

"About how I can get more funds released."

"Funds released? For what?"

"For the fencing around the old church for one thing. After last night, there's one thing we can agree on and that's that the fencing isn't anywhere near secure enough. The work to do it properly can't wait on Father O'Neil."

"You'll have to discuss that with the Bishop."

Devlin leaned back in his chair and sighed. "I intend to. In the meantime, I need to see the accounts, Susan. I want to see how much is in the sink fund and how much extra I need to ask the Bishop for."

Susan looked uncomfortable and avoided Devlin's gaze.

"You can't refuse me, Susan."

Susan pursed her lips, her eyes flitting around the coffee shop then back onto Devlin. "You do know the kids that broke into the old church were from Avery High? No doubt the same kids doing that project and climbing all over the cemetery this morning."

"Did Father O'Neil tell you not to let me see the church accounts, Susan?"

"Not in so many words."

"So what's the problem?"

"He... He said he didn't trust you. That you didn't know how to run a church. That I... I was to protect it for him... For Father O'Neil."

"Right now, I run Holy Cross and only I am responsible for it. And, if you don't hand the accounts over, I will formally ask you to step down from your position as the financial officer."

Susan's face reddened with anger. The position on the church council was a source of great pride and being 'formally asked' to step down had all the hallmarks of a small-town scandal. Despite all of this she remained calm. She took a sip of her tea and nodded primly.

"I'll email the files over to you."

"I want the files going back ten years at least."

"Ten...?"

"It's no good giving me this years', or the last few years. I need to get the whole picture."

"But you're not really going to look at ten years' worth of accounts?"

"If I say I want ten years' of accounts then I mean I'm going to look at ten years' of accounts. I have to talk to the Bishop about securing the old church and I have to be fully informed before I have that conversation."

"It's a lot of work. A *lot* of work."

"I can wait."

"You'll have to."

They finished their drinks and made very small talk. Susan's manner had turned cold to the point of being rude. Once the bill was settled, they both rose to leave without speaking.

Outside, the wind was sharp and the cold bit hard. Susan was wrapped in a fur-lined puffa and Devlin had the collars of his overcoat up around his chin. As they stepped onto the sidewalk Susan's attention was caught by a man loitering by a parked car, a sports model Lexus sedan. The man had seen Susan too. He nodded and came over.

"Susan. How are you?" The man was neatly dressed in a gray tweed coat. His black hair was carefully parted and slicked back, and his beard was just as carefully trimmed, and just as black.

"Hello, Adam," replied Susan. "I'm good, thank you."

"Good, good."

There was a stiff formality between the two. Devlin was about to make his excuses, but a flustered Susan seemed to feel obliged to introduce the two men.

"This is Father Devlin. He's looking after Holy Cross while Father O'Neil is convalescing. Father, this is Adam Berry."

"Good to meet you, Father."

"Likewise."

"Adam is the Schools Superintendent for Worcester. He sits on the Board of Education and Father O'Neil sits on the school's committee."

"That's right," said Berry cheerfully. "How are you settling in at Holy Cross, Father?"

"I'm finding my feet okay."

"Glad to hear it."

Sensing some vague awkwardness between them, Devlin made his excuses and left Susan and Berry standing on the sidewalk. He walked a little way, but curiosity got the better of him and he glanced back. Susan had folded her arms and was looking at the ground, while Adam Berry seemed to be agitated, remonstrating with her. Devlin briefly wondered what had gotten Berry so fired up. He had to get back to Holy Cross for the Sacrament of Reconciliation, however, so he dismissed the scene as small-town politics and headed to his car.

BY THE TIME Devlin arrived back at Holy Cross, he had only half an hour before the Sacrament of Reconciliation began. He left the rectory and stopped for a moment to look over toward the fenced overgrown field where the old church stood. Winter had stripped the landscape to the bones and had covered what was left with a mist. Through the bare trees, Devlin thought he could see a strip of police tape. And, as he stood squinting into the distance, he saw a short, compact man in a bulky flight jacket coming toward him. It was Detective Sergeant Ted Hennessy, and the closer he got the redder his face became from exertion and cold air. It wasn't long before the Detective was in front of him, panting from the walk, and puffing out jets of condensation.

"Father, I wanted to give you an update. We've excavated the body and the boys from the Bureau are finishing up. We should have the scene finished with by tonight."

"Thanks for letting me know. Did you find anything useful?"

"Well, forensics say they think the skeleton looks like it was a boy, a teenager, around puberty."

"Do they know how old the body is?"

"Yeah. They said what you said, about the teeth fillings being less than fifty years old. Or at least some forensic guy just out of diapers did. The body had to have been buried after the church had been closed down. How did you know about that fillings thing?"

"After I was a pararescue I was an Air Force detective. We pretty much had to take on anything and everything, including homicide. We had a cold case, a body found during building work in Pope Field. It turned out to be an old missing person case, a US Air Force staff sergeant who had been killed in a fight with another sergeant on the base. Quickest and cheapest way we had to establish time of death was one filling in his back teeth that quickly dated the body as modern and not, say, a Civil War soldier."

Hennessy pursed his lips and gave Devlin a sideways look. "Well, ain't you a box of surprises? I wouldn't go telling anyone until we get lab results on the bone. It won't be all that accurate, but it should give us a window of about ten years. It is looking pretty certain this is foul play. I think it's a matter of time before this is officially classed as a homicide."

THE SACRAMENT of Reconciliation took up the whole afternoon, with the last of the parishioners finishing their confession at five o'clock. Alone in the confessional, Devlin took a moment to himself, listening to penance being muttered outside and shortly after the sound of the parishioner leaving the church.

He stepped out of the confessional hoping for empty pews and total solitude. A church to himself. However, he found he was not alone. Sitting in a pew toward the back of the church was a figure with their head bowed. The visitor's head sprung up, and he smiled at Devlin.

"Hello, Father." The eyes were bright and the voice was too.

"Father Deeney," said Devlin.

"Come join me, Father."

Devlin accepted the invitation and sat beside Deeney. Devlin was struck again by Deeney's appearance. He looked like a man who had spent his life in manual work rather than cosseted in the priesthood. In fact, thought Devlin, Deeney and he were in some ways very similar.

"What brings you to Holy Cross?" asked Devlin.

"Oh, I like the church here. I like the feel of the place. I often drive past on my way from St. Mary's going out of town. On my way back, if I have five minutes I'll stop to sit and pray. In some ways, I prefer it to St. Mary's. How're you settling in?"

"I'm having a push and pull with the Bishop and Father O'Neil over what I can and can't do, though I think I'm on my way to smoothing that out."

"Good. What will you do after Father O'Neil comes back?"

"I really don't know."

Deeney seemed to consider Devlin's reply and for a moment they were both silent.

"I heard about the body in the old church," said Deeney.

"Word really does get around fast here."

"Well, not a lot happens. So when it does, it gets around. Was it a burial?"

"No. I had a look over the burial records for the old church and there was no plot in the crypt."

"Those records though? Are they completely reliable?"

"Maybe not."

"The last burial in the old plot had to be seventy years ago. I mean, it's like ancient history back there. You know the story? Why they haven't found a way to clear it?"

"I thought it was money."

"Yes, it's money." Deeney leaned closer to Devlin, somewhat conspiratorially. "There's an important family in Avery, very rich. The Driscolls. Big donors to the Diocese. They have a mausoleum back in the old church and a row of plots. Graves of great-grandparents and great-great-grandparents who came over from the old country. They paid for the new church way-back-when and they won't let the old cemetery go." Deeney, still leaning in toward Devlin, raised an eyebrow and Devlin noticed that there were tiny dark spots on the chest of his otherwise immaculate tunic. "The irony is they aren't great churchgoers," Deeney continued. "The head of the family is a thug called Tony Driscoll. Hard-drinking and quick-tempered."

"I've met him. Married his son and daughter-in-law the other day. We didn't get on."

"But here am I gossiping. Don't let me keep you if you have somewhere to be."

"I HAVE to meet with the church committee at five and I have matters before that I want to see to."

"I understand. Busy time."

"Yeah. Busy time."

"You know," said Deeney with a flash of earnestness. "Even though I hardly know you, Father, I admire you. I get a real sense that you are a man carved out of faith. Someone who doesn't shrink from their destiny. I know you spent some time searching, out on the road. I like that. It's unconventional. So did I. I spent time in a spiritual wilderness. Without a church. Looking for my destiny." Deeney suddenly laid a hand on Devlin's arm and his tone changed. "But I sense something in you. A turbulence. A profound disruption, like a breach in your spirit. Even, dare I say it, like a demon."

For a moment, Devlin was lost for words. Here was a man who had no knowledge of Devlin's past yet had somehow seemed to put his finger on Devlin's most fundamental struggle. And the effect was physical too. The place where Deeney had laid his hand on Devlin's arm felt suddenly cold, and the chill began to creep up his arm and throughout his upper body.

"And I think, Father," Deeney continued, "that I can help you. I can set that demon free."

Then, without waiting for an answer, Deeney stood.

"Have a productive committee. I very much look forward to our next meeting."

Deeney departed, leaving Devlin reeling. In the absolute silence of the church a voice came back to Devlin, a voice he had been carrying with him. It was the voice of a dying man, Professor Zhou, who had told him that one day he would meet someone who would free him. Free him from guilt. Free him from Felix Lemus's curse; that wherever Devlin went, evil would come for him. Devlin suddenly had the extraordinary thought that perhaps Professor Zhou's prophesy might be right. That maybe he had just met the person who would set him free.

Devlin checked his watch and saw he still had some time before the committee meeting. He rose and walked the length of the aisle, crossed in front of the first row of seats, and walked toward an arched wooden door in the transept wall. He felt for a heavy metal key in his pocket, drew it out, then inserted it into the lock and turned it. The door opened, letting out an icy, damp gust of wind from the bowels of the building.

Devlin flicked a switch on the wall, lighting his way down the narrow stone staircase into the Holy Cross crypt. Though it was damp and cold, unlike the one under the old church this crypt had signs of recent and ongoing use. Mainly it was where Tanner, the sexton, kept his tools, old headstones in need of repair, and new ones waiting to be set. The space was close to overcrowded with all the bits and pieces stowed away out of sight.

Three naked bulbs hung from the low, vaulted ceiling, providing barely enough light to see. On the far side of the crypt

was a row of wooden boxes stacked on each other. The boxes at
the top almost touched the brickwork overhead.

Devlin had been here once before since he came to Holy
Cross, so he knew which box he was after. It was a box marked
with an orange plastic label embossed with the words 'Holy
Cross Burial Plots.' It lay on the floor, separate from the other
records.

For a moment Devlin surveyed the rickety sum of the church
archives. It struck Devlin that this mound of boxes was like
everything else at Holy Cross, ramshackle and make-do. Yet, the
state of neglect seemed to Devlin more out of purpose than
neglect. As if someone wanted the past to lie uninspected in a
corner gathering mold. Maybe, in the end, it was only Father
O'Neil who knew everything about Holy Cross.

Devlin knelt and lifted out the scroll that lay on top. The last
scroll to be placed in the box. In the top corner, it was dated with
a "1945" stamp. There was a compass by the date, and drawn
below were lines that marked out the boundaries of a field.
Within the field, just off from the center, was a simple
rectangular plan of the old church. On the north and south sides
of the church were rows of crosses which signified the positions
of graves. Everything on the scroll was drawn in a black ink that
had faded and aged. Devlin scanned the scroll to confirm what
he remembered to be true; that there was no burial plot
recorded within the walls of the church, only in the outside
grounds.

From up above, through the open door to the crypt, came
the sound of wind blowing hard. The bulbs flickered on and off
and Devlin had the strangest feeling, that this place, a place of
God, had witnessed Godless acts.

Out in the hard night, ravens croaked, and leaves tumbled
across the path from the church back to the rectory. A low fog
had settled. As Devlin rounded the corner of the church he

made out someone standing outside the rectory door. Looking harder through the mist he realized the figure was bent low and seemed to be trying to force the door.

Devlin's pace began to quicken into a run, but before he could gain speed the figure looked up and saw Devlin approaching. The person sprinted off, heading diagonally across the cemetery. Devlin gave chase through headstones and murky fog. He was quick but his quarry was now fast enough and close enough to the road to disappear over the fence that ran along the perimeter of the church grounds. By the time Devlin had reached the fence, he could already hear an engine starting. Leaping the fence and landing on a strip of grass on the other side, he watched as the tail lights of a car vanished over the brow of the hill and into the night.

Devlin retraced his steps back to the house and went through the mechanics of reporting the incident to the police. A dispatcher took the details and a cruiser arrived an hour or so later. The door was treated for prints and Devlin answered all the cop's questions. Yet, it was clear there was nowhere to go with the whole thing.

"Maybe think about CCTV?" suggested the officer as he got back in his car.

"I hear you," replied Devlin, knowing full well it was unlikely to happen on his watch.

Gallagher's Tavern was located in a midtown mall. If you lived in Avery you'd probably driven past it many times without noticing it. That was what Detective Ted Hennessy liked about the place. Okay, so the service wasn't the best and the pulled pork sandwich sitting on the bar in front of him was swimming in grease. But the place was quiet, so you could follow the game and you weren't going to run into people you knew.

Tonight though, Gallagher's wasn't quite so peaceful. The main bar was empty apart from Hennessy and a couple of other guys. But the back room had been hired out privately and from the sounds of cheers and laughter it was bursting at the seams.

Hennessy took a bite of his sandwich, washed it down with a gulp of beer, and watched the action play out on the big screen on the wall. The Bills were running it close against the Patriots in the last quarter and Hennessy, who had money on the Patriots, was on the edge of his barstool.

He was so engrossed in the game that he didn't notice the door to the backroom open and a member of the private party come into the main bar.

"Detective?"

Hennessy, startled to hear his professional title being used, swiveled around on his stool with a mouth full of pulled pork. Standing right by him, leaning on the bar and grinning broadly, was Tony Driscoll.

"Well, well. So this is where you hide out from DUIs and the old lady."

"Tony? What are you doing here?"

"One of the fellas in the firm is retiring. Been driving trucks for the family for thirty years. We're throwing a big party for him and the other drivers. Free bar. But that's the problem. I can't get an order in back there." Driscoll pulled out his wallet and laid it on the bar. "Gonna be a big night, Ted. Maybe later we'll hit a strip joint over in Worcester. Say, why don't you join us?"

"That's a kind offer, Tony, but I ain't got money to throw down a G-string."

Driscoll laughed and slapped Hennessy hard on the back. "Oh, c'mon, for Christ's sake. I'd stand you a dance or two. What d'ya say?"

"Be a great night, Tone. But I got the old lady waiting at home for me. I can't be heading off to Worcester."

"That's a real shame. I'm sorry about that, Ted. Real sorry."

"I'm sorry too. You know how it is, anything to keep things sweet back home."

"Sounds like you're a man under the thumb, detective." Driscoll gestured to the bar tender and ordered a Macallan's on the rocks. "So tell me, what's all this with a body being discovered at the old church?"

"All we know is there's a skeleton of a teenage boy that was buried there maybe decades ago."

"After the old church shutdown?"

"Yeah."

"So is it murder?"

"We don't know for sure."

Driscoll shook his head and whistled. "Murder in Avery. Unbelievable. What about this Father Devlin? What's his story?"

"Seems okay. Ex-Air Force, pararescue. Seen some action I'd say."

Driscoll nodded again. His drink had arrived and he sipped at it. "You know what I heard?"

"What?"

"He had some kind of mental breakdown. Left his last church in a hurry."

"That so?"

"It is. I also heard he has a hard time keeping his drinking in check. Big old booze hound."

"Well, I guess a man can change."

Driscoll laughed. "Yes he can detective, yes he can. Though I always find those that say they've changed, inside, they're on a twenty-four-hour alert, guarding against the dreadful temptation to change back." Driscoll laid a hand on Hennessy's shoulder. "You look after yourself, Ted, and send my regards to the ol' ball and chain." Then he drifted off with his drink, detouring around the bar to talk to the bar tender before disappearing into the backroom that was still rocking with shouts and laughter.

Hennessy beckoned over the bar tender and asked to settle up.

"Oh," said the bar tender, a little surprised. "Your bill's already settled. Mr. Driscoll paid it on his tab."

"No." Hennessy placed thirty dollars on the bar. "Take it off his bill thank you. This will cover it."

"Sure. Of course."

Hennessy slid off his stool and looked up at the screen. The Bills were up 24-21 and the Buffalo's quarterback had fumbled a pass with thirty seconds to go.

"Great," he mumbled. "Just great."

As he left there was a roar of laughter from the backroom. Hennessy felt suddenly queasy. And it wasn't because of the pulled-pork sandwich.

12

Sarah woke with a gasp, as if she had just managed to break the surface of the sea and could finally fill her lungs with air. For a terrifyingly long time she wasn't sure either who she was, or where. It was like she had just been born.

She had been dreaming of being buried alive, earth in her mouth, down her throat, on her eyeballs. Then she had struggled free and, like before, she saw the night sky come and go and tree tops bloom and wither. Finally she saw the yellow snakes. Or at least what looked like seven yellow snakes that had had their tails bound in a rope.

She realized that she was in her apartment, lying alone on her couch. And her heart broke all over again. She looked at the clock on the wall. It was just past eight in the evening. She must have fallen asleep after coming back from school. She felt her forehead, and found it damp. She got up and splashed cold water over her face and rubbed it off with a towel. She went to the kitchen and poured herself a glass of milk, then sat on the couch with her knees up under her chin.

She was experiencing some kind of existential crisis, she was sure. She'd just broken up with the person she thought she'd be with for the rest of her life, the person she was going to have children with, grandchildren with. Now all that had vanished and had yet to be replaced. Maybe could never be replaced. She was at a crossroads that would define the rest of her life, and when a person is at such a crossroads they become vulnerable, unstable, and overwhelmed by the significance of where they are.

"C'mon Sarah, get a grip for crying out loud. It'll be okay. Give it a month or so and I'll be fine. I just need to keep my head."

She found her cell wedged between the cushions, sat cross-legged on the couch, and was about to start looking for therapists in Boston when the buzzer went. She padded over to the intercom and pressed the button.

"Hi..."

"Sarah?"

"Mom?"

Sarah's mom stood just inside the doorway and took it all in. The one-bed apartment, the minimal furniture, and no fiancée.

"How did you find my address?" Sarah found herself asking for the second time in as many days.

"Theresa told me. She told me everything. I know you swore her to secrecy but she felt she had to tell me, your mother. What happened, Sarah?"

"I'm sorry. I should have told you before... And I was going to... It was just... too painful..."

"You really shouldn't hold these things back from me. It's not right... or fair on me, to keep secrets. I'm your mother and I should know what's happening in my daughter's life... Are you okay, Sarah, really?"

She wasn't okay, but she knew better than to unload on her mom who would end up more upset than Sarah and be the one needing consoling. "I'm doing okay, y'know. Okay. Come in."

Sarah served up coffee and a plate of cookies, and they sat with their mugs at either end of the couch.

"Maybe I'm just a bad picker," said Sarah. "I mean, you remember that guy I lived with in Boston? Jason?"

"You mean the drug dealer?"

"Small-time drug dealer. And I didn't even know about it till the cops raided our apartment. Sheesh. Maybe I just have a talent for picking the wrong guy."

"You know, Sarah," said her mom, changing the subject, "if you need money it's not a problem."

"No. The one thing that's going smoothly at the moment is work. I think I may be asked to apply for Head of the History Department."

"That's good. Sweetheart, you look tired."

Sarah winced. For her mom, appearances mattered. "I haven't been sleeping great. I've been having the craziest dreams."

"What dreams?"

"Oh, it's too dull to go into detail. It all started when I went to see a medium..."

"A medium? Why on earth...?"

"It was a whim. Nothing serious. Or so I thought. The medium started gabbling on about seeing another face in mine. Like there was someone else inside me. I mean, I figured it was nonsense. But since then I've had the strangest dreams. And the more I think about it the more I feel... This is crazy I know... That she really did see something,"

Her mother picked up a cookie and nibbled at it. For some reason, she seemed to be agitated, even angry. Sarah wondered if mentioning the medium had somehow freaked her out.

"What do you think?" asked Sarah.

"Like you said, I think it's nonsense. Ridiculous nonsense. The medium suggested something deliberately wishy-washy so she could reel you in. Into some made-up mystical story. Somehow that's caught your imagination. Sometimes, Sarah, you're in danger of being away with the fairies. You need to keep your feet on solid ground. You need to be more like your sister."

There was so much more Sarah could have told her mother, but she just wasn't the right audience. Instead she nodded politely and bit her lip. Her mother leaned forward and put a hand on her knee. She wasn't a tactile person, so this was the closest she came to affection.

"You're going through a very difficult time and it's clearly affecting you in all sorts of ways. But I'm here and so is Theresa. We're both here for you." She took her hand off Sarah's knee and glanced around the apartment. "Now. This place could do with brightening up. How about you look for some new furniture? And drapes, and cushions? Whatever you like, and I'll pay for it."

"That would be really nice. Thank you."

Her mother put a hand back on Sarah's knee. "It'll be alright, Sarah. It'll be alright."

Sarah smiled and nodded, yet in her heart she wasn't at all sure it was going to be alright. Her dreams were getting more vivid and disturbing, and something had to be done about it.

13

It wasn't a long trip, just over an hour heading south on the interstate. But it was a filthy November day, gray and flat. It was cold too, as if snow was trying to will itself into existence but without any luck.

Sarah came off the interstate and hooked around east on the 28 till she found the signs she was looking for.

Edaville Theme Park was as busy as it was the day she had visited with her sister and the kids. She resented the entry fee, but at least this time she knew exactly where she was going and how to get there. She got her bearings again using the primary-colored theme park map, then cut across the fairground until she came to the old cabin in which Amber Luna plied her trade. The events that had taken place in the cabin seemed almost unreal now. After all, the only witnesses were her and a complete stranger she had met just once. Yet, coming back to see the cabin felt like a positive thing, something concrete among all the goddamn dreams she was having.

The only problem was that the cabin was still there, but Amber Luna wasn't. The door was locked and there was no sign of life.

She stood by the cabin for a while, not knowing what to do next. Then she spotted one of the theme park helpers, a girl in her early twenties, maybe younger, with a radio clutched in her hand and dressed in a florescent jacket.

"Hey, excuse me. Could you help me?"

"Sure," said the girl.

"I was looking for Amber Luna, the mystic. She doesn't seem to be around."

The girl frowned and replied with a non-committal, "Right..."

"Do you know where she is?"

"No. I haven't seen her for a few days. Think the hut's been locked since Sunday. She might even have left for good."

"You don't know where I could find her?"

"'Fraid not. The thing is, she isn't really anything to do with us. To be honest, we don't really even know how she came to be here. I think she rents the hut because no one else will take it. Our job is to look after the rides and the customers. Amber Luna is kind of an oddity we sort of... ignore. Sorry." The girl headed off and then swiveled around, talking to Sarah as she was backing away. "But you could google her. I heard she runs her business out of where she lives, when she isn't doing it here."

"Okay. Thanks."

Sarah took her cell out and googled 'Amber Luna mystic' and, thanks to the unique nature of the name, she got a hit immediately. Up came a cheap-looking website with a photo of Amber from some years ago. On the contact page was an address in Plymouth Bay.

IT WAS LESS than a twenty-minute drive to the address, a plain-looking apartment block off a deserted highway on the outskirts of Plymouth. Sarah took a turn-off into the parking lot, then got out of her car and went looking for Amber Luna's apartment, which turned out to be a condo on the top floor. There was no buzzer, just a door that opened into a lobby with mailboxes along the wall. The stairs and hallway smelled of cigarettes and air freshener. Pretty much everything needed care and attention; paint peeling off the walls, windows cracked, carpets faded and worn.

Sarah found the right apartment and knocked. She heard the sound of feet marching to the door. The footsteps stopped and there was a pause, during which Sarah guessed she was being eyed up and down through the peep hole. Then the door opened to reveal Amber Luna, not looking so deserving of her exotic name. She was dressed in sweatpants and a baggy 'Wicked' T-shirt. Hair that had been carefully shaped when Sarah had first met her was flat and wild. Amber Luna leaned on the door frame with her arms folded. Her eyes were glazed and her cheeks were flushed.

"Hi," said Sarah. "I don't know if you remember me...?"

"Oh, I remember you."

"Oh, good, great. That's great. I was wondering if I could talk to you about the consultation you did for me?"

"I'm off duty."

"Oh." Amber Luna's teeth and lips were red with wine and there was a strong smell of grass coming from the apartment. "Well, if I paid you...?"

"I said I was off duty."

"... and to make up for the inconvenience I could pay you double."

Amber Luna's heavily mascaraed eyes narrowed. "It's more of an inconvenience than that."

"How much?"

"Triple. It's triple the inconvenience."

"Okay, then. Triple."

"You have cash?"

"Yeah, I do."

"Then come on in."

Sarah followed Amber into the living room, where a large glass of red wine and a nearly empty bottle stood on the coffee table. Country music was whining out of a laptop. A stubbed-out joint lay in an ash tray on the floor by the slider that led to the balcony.

Amber sat in an armchair and Sarah sat on the couch. It was clear that this consultation was going to be very different from the first.

"You don't mind if I drink, do you?" asked Amber.

"No. Not at all." Sarah neither expected nor wanted to be offered a drink.

Amber took a gulp of wine and licked her lips. "Money up front please."

"Oh, yeah." Sarah took out her purse and counted out the cash then placed it on the coffee table.

"What can I do for you?"

"This is going to sound a bit weird. Well, maybe not to you, maybe this is usual to you. But your consultation really freaked me out."

Amber Luna shifted in her armchair, looking uncomfortable. She took another sip of wine.

"And the thing is, since we met I've been having weird things happening to me. I've had the weirdest dreams. Dreams that just won't quit. Dreams that started after I saw you and are linked to what you said to me."

Amber Luna didn't reply.

"And I wondered what you thought about that?"

"What I thought about it?"

"Yeah, what do you think it means?"

Amber rolled the wine in her glass around. "I think it's probably just your imagination."

"That's it? It's my imagination. That's your consultation?"

"That's it. That's my consultation."

"I thought you were a medium. I thought you could talk to the spirits."

"When there are spirits I talk to spirits. When it's someone's overactive imagination, I tell them it's their overactive imagination."

"But you said you saw something in my face, someone else."

"Trick of the light."

"Trick of the light?"

"Trick of the light."

"Wow. Okay. Well, this has been an expensive disappointment."

Amber shrugged and her large bust rose and fell. "It is what it is."

"Right."

For a moment Sarah didn't speak, and the longer the silence went on the more uneasy Amber became.

Finally, Sarah said, "I don't believe you."

Amber shrugged again.

"You did see something. I know you did."

"You've had your consultation. You can leave now."

"No. I'm not leaving. You saw something. I know it." Sarah leaned forward and took a swig from the wine bottle. It was cheap and sharp but it warmed her up.

"Hey, that's just rude..."

"Why weren't you at the place in Edaville?"

"What? I'm on vacation. Business was slow."

"I spoke to someone who works there and they said you hadn't been at Edaville since Sunday."

"So?"

"That's the day I went to see you."

"So?"

"What did you see, Amber?"

"My name isn't Amber. It's Lucy."

"No kidding, Lucy." Sarah took another bigger gulp from the wine bottle for more courage.

"Hey, screw you. Stop drinking my wine."

"I'll stop drinking it when you answer my question. What did you see last week in your hut in Edaville? And I swear, I'm not leaving until you tell me because it's *that* important to me."

"I'll call the cops."

"Call the cops. I'll make such a racket, I'll resist and scream and bite and kick, and you'll have a lot of explaining to do to the neighbors and the landlord. I'm a crazy woman, I really am." Sarah took one more gulp of wine and slammed the bottle down on the table. "Now tell me what you saw and your life will be a whole lot easier."

Amber's eyes were bloodshot and she seemed to waver back and forth in her chair, the wine and weed taking powerful effect.

"Lucy...?" said Sarah, suddenly concerned for her host's health.

"I feel sick. Get me a glass of water... please... I need some water."

Sarah filled a glass with tap water and gave it to Lucy, who gulped it in one then proffered the empty glass back up to Sarah. "Another... please... Then I'll tell you...."

One more glass of water seemed to stabilize Lucy. She lit up a cigarette and nodded toward the ceiling. "Took the batteries out of the smoke detectors."

"Right. How're you feeling?"

Lucy stood, steadied herself, blew out a line of smoke, and said, "I wanna show you something. God knows I gotta show someone..."

Sarah followed Lucy back along the corridor to a bedroom. Lucy pushed open the door.

"Go in, take a look."

Tentatively, Sarah stepped into the room. There was a double bed, a rack of clothes, and a TV in the corner. Most of the room and walls were covered in pieces of paper. On every piece of paper were pencil drawings of a face. The features were blurred, indistinct. Some pictures were a little clearer than others, as if the artist was trying to get closer to a clear picture of a face that remained stubbornly out of focus. But it was a male face. In some of the sketches, the hair and eyes had been colored in black and green.

"Like I said, my name's Lucy, not Amber. And I was a big old fake psychic. Till I met you."

"These drawings... Who is it?"

"It's all I see now since you came for a reading. All I see. In my dreams, when I wake, in the faces of other people."

"Who is it?"

"I wish I goddamn knew."

14

Devlin was still chewing over his encounter with Bishop Molina and Father O'Neil when he pulled up in front of the rectory. Yet all of that vanished when he got out of the car and noticed the rectory door was slightly ajar. Devlin stopped dead, placed a hand on the door, and gently pushed it open a few more inches so he could slip into the hall. Light spilled from the kitchen doorway and Devlin braced himself to confront whoever had been trying to break into the rectory. Fists clenched, he entered the kitchen and there, standing expectantly, waiting for Devlin by the kitchen table, was a tall, slender man with a stoop. In his sixties but still mostly dark-haired, the visitor, dressed in a suit and clerical collar, clapped his hands and stamped his feet.

"You're late, Gabe, and it's too damn cold to be stood around."

"How did you get in?"

"Your sexton, Tanner, let me in out of respect for my title and fear of my old age."

"Cardinal Hermes," replied Devlin, smiling. "This is an honor."

"You can drop the title. It's just Hector to you, Gabe."

"Really good to see you, Hector."

"Good to see you too. Now, get some coffee going and tell me everything you've found out about Holy Cross."

Devlin heated some coffee up on the stove and served them a mug each. Then he left the kitchen and returned with a folder under his arm. Beneath the low-beamed roof of the rectory kitchen, the two men settled in around the old mahogany table.

"I got a call from the Bishop this morning," said Hermes. "About a body found on the grounds of the old church."

"What did he tell you?"

"He told me the police are involved. That he thinks it's an unrecorded official burial. But he mostly spent the call complaining about you and your idea that it's suspicious."

"It's not just my idea. It's a homicide, and that's likely to be official when the lab results come back. The local detective told me as much. And even if he hadn't, I'd still think it was a homicide."

"Why?"

"The skeleton showed signs of strangulation. The way the body was buried, shallow, diagonally, out of line with the walls of the church. It just doesn't look like a church burial."

"Couldn't there have been ground movement? It's an old, dilapidated building. Abandoned and crumbling."

"No. From what I saw, I'd bet the shirt on my back that it was a homicide. And the local detective on the case is pretty sure that's where it's going too."

"That's extraordinary, isn't it? A murder victim found on church property."

"Yeah, it is. Though, it may just have been a convenient place to dump the body."

"I'll have my office call Avery PD. So far the Bishop's office has been handling it. If it is homicide like you say it is, I'll need to take a lead on it." Hermes took a sip from his mug, peering at the folder that Devlin had brought into the kitchen and was now laid in front of him. He interlinked his fingers on the table and leaned forward.

"So, Gabe. What's the story?"

Devlin pushed the folder across the table toward Hermes.

"Last ten years of accounts. Just like you asked for. I only got them this morning."

"Excellent. Was it difficult?" Hermes opened the folder and began flicking through its contents.

"I encountered some resistance."

"From Father O'Neil?"

"No. I don't think he's aware I have them. Susan Hennessy, the finance secretary, she gave them to me after I point blank demanded them. They've been trying to keep me out of any serious church business here since I arrived. I'd say the Bishop and Father O'Neil made that decision together before I got here. It's pretty clear they don't trust me."

Hermes looked up and raised an eyebrow. "Well, they were right not to."

"Given the icy reception I've had, I really don't know how you managed to force me on them."

"I just flat out insisted. Being a Cardinal does bring quite some clout with it."

"Couldn't you have demanded the accounts yourself?"

"I could have, yes. But it's unheard of for a Cardinal to go over the Bishop's Office head and request individual church accounts without clear evidence of fraud. I wanted to find a less heavy-handed way that wouldn't arouse suspicion. And I wanted to see the raw accounts, not something cooked up for my eyes." Hermes clasped Devlin's hand. "Thanks for getting hold of this." Hermes returned to skimming the accounts in front of him.

"What is it you're looking for?"

"I don't know exactly. All I know is that, like I told you,

someone in the Bishop's office blew the whistle. They sent an anonymous tip-off. Said the accounts from Holy Cross were unusually vague and contained irregularities."

"Such as?"

"The church's available funds had dropped year on year but there was no material reason why this should be the case. Holy Cross has a few wealthy donors who continue to contribute fairly generously. The congregation numbers, small as they are, remained the same, other streams of income are the same, so where's the leak? Things came to a head when the Archdiocesan Finance Council received an emergency request for capital funds to address failing infrastructure at Holy Cross."

"So, you think Father O'Neil's skimming?"

"I believe the legal term is defalcation. But yes, in essence, he may be, as you say, 'skimming.'"

"Then where's the money going? I've only been here a short while but as far as I can see Father O'Neil has a pretty frugal life-style. I mean, just take a look around the place."

"That's the problem. I can't see where the cash would be going."

"Unless he's salting it away in some pension pot."

"Possibly."

"That's a copy by the way. You can take it with you,"

Hermes closed the folder and smiled. "You've done a great job, Gabe. Just like I knew you would."

"It's the least I could do, after all the help you gave me. After the hell you went through because of me and the stuff in Halton Springs."

Hermes smiled and flexed his hand. "They fixed my hand up okay. It doesn't ache too much. Let's forgive the past and not dwell on it."

"Thank you, Hector."

Hermes stood, pulled his jacket off the back of the chair he'd been sitting in, and put it on.

"Like I said, you've done a great job."

"So that's it?"

"No. I'll ask our accountants to look this over. You keep an eye on things here. You're my man on the ground now Gabe."

15

Devlin mingled among the small groups of churchgoers loitering in the vestibule, a convenient nook out of the cold. It was an opportunity after Mass for Devlin to make contact face-to-face and maybe slowly win acceptance. The difficulty was that all people wanted to know about was the body found in the old crypt. Thus, getting past that into meaningful conversation was proving nearly impossible. Added to that was a feeling Devlin was beginning to get from the parishioners at Holy Cross. A feeling that they didn't trust him, perhaps were even a little afraid of him.

As the church emptied of the last of the worshipers, Devlin spotted the stout, round figure of the Detective Sergeant Ted Hennessy approaching. The people heading for their cars all slowed and rubbernecked Hennessy, then exchanged knowing looks.

"Father Devlin."

"Detective. I'm guessing you have news."

"I do. Could we go somewhere a little more private?"

Devlin took Hennessy to the rectory where they settled into the living room. Hennessy perched himself on the couch, leaning forward a little, ready to address Devlin who was sitting opposite in an armchair.

"You were right, Father. Forensics say the body isn't more than ten to twenty years old. Nowhere near old enough to be a burial. It's the skeleton of a boy, teenage, early teenage they think. The damage to the hyoid bone and the vertebrae is consistent with strangulation. Homicide in Worcester is opening a murder case. They're sending detectives out to interview Father O'Neil. Even if the body is twenty years old, the timing means it happened while he was priest here. I said go easy on him, given the cancer operation and everything. And, let's face it, Father O'Neil is no murderer. He couldn't kill a fly, let alone a person. However, the thing is, we don't have any leads on who the victim was. No record of anyone local going missing, no match on dental records."

"You think it's a lost cause, don't you detective?"

"I'm no homicide cop but we're a long way out from the golden hour, wouldn't you say, Father?"

"Yes, we are."

"The homicide boys wanted to take a look at the old church records. If there are any. I said I'd talk to you about it."

"There are records but they're not well kept. They're in the crypt here, just boxed up really. Any time they want to come take a look, they can. I have a set of keys and so does Hoyt Tanner, the sexton."

The detective rubbed the thinning blond hair that fanned his crown. "Hell of a business. You must have a strange idea about Avery, Father. I have to tell you, I've lived here all my life and this town is a nothing-ever-happens-kind-of-place."

"I guess I'm just unlucky."

"Unlucky is right. Susan, she's freaked out by the whole thing. Just a bag of nerves."

"That's perfectly understandable."

The conversation stalled for a moment and Hennessy seemed to be working up to saying something.

"What is it, detective?"

"Father, would you take a word of advice from someone who knows the bones of this town, if you'll excuse the unfortunate turn of phrase?"

"I'd welcome it."

"There's some talk here, about the things that have happened since you've arrived. The talk is that it all started happening when you came to Avery. That there's something about you, Father Devlin. Something that attracts bad things."

"What's the advice, detective?"

"Excuse me?"

"You said you had some advice for me. What you've said is very interesting, but I wouldn't class it as advice. At least any advice I could use."

"I apologize. Maybe it was more an observation than advice." Hennessy glanced down at his watch. "Shoot, I better get going. I got a meet with the boys out of Worcester back at the station." He stood and straightened himself out. "I'll let them know they can swing by and take a look at the records."

"Before you go, I wanted to mention something. A few days ago I noticed the front door seemed to have been forced. I reported it to an officer at the station. Last night, I caught someone trying to break into the rectory. They were trying to force the front door open. I chased them across the cemetery but they got away, in a car. A cruiser came out and took details."

"Can I take a look at the front door?"

Devlin and Hennessy went out front and Devlin watched the detective examine the front door. It was already getting dark, so Hennessy had to get up close and use his flashlight.

"Yeah, sure looks like someone tried to jimmy this. You get a look at the guy? Any kind of description?"

"No. It was dark and there was a lot of fog. They were male, around average height, dark hair. I didn't get close enough for a good description."

Hennessy looked around the front of the rectory.

"You should get some CCTV installed here. That's what you should do." he swung back to Devlin. "Could've been a kid trying their luck. Susan was telling me you had kids from Avery High down here. Maybe that isn't such a good idea. Encouraging them to hang out here."

"It wasn't a kid."

"You said you couldn't tell much about him."

"I could tell it wasn't a kid and they were at least old enough to drive."

"Okay. But I'd put CCTV in here. That's the first thing I'd do."

"Due to me being the temporary priest here, I'm afraid I don't have those funds at my disposal, detective. Your wife will know all about that."

Hennessy shrugged. "I don't get involved in all of that... politics, Father. If that's all, I'll take my leave." Hennessy began to walk back to his cruiser.

"Oh, and, detective," Devlin called out. "If you can keep me posted about the investigation. I'm sure the Bishop will want to know how it's going."

"Naturally," replied Hennessy without turning back.

Once Hennessy had gone Devlin went into the rectory and checked his diary. He was conscious there were house calls he needed to make. He was about to ring around to arrange appointments when he heard a knock at the door.

A little frustrated about being stopped from chipping away at routine business, Devlin closed his diary and went to the door. Standing on the stoop was the Avery High teacher, Sarah Wilson.

"Hello, Father.

"Hello. Can I help you?"

"Would you have a moment to help a woman who thinks she might be losing her mind?"

DEVLIN SUGGESTED THEY TAKE A WALK. Wrapped in thick coats and scarves, they cut through the cemetery, crossed the road into Avery, and began walking through the adjoining field.

"I hope you don't mind me taking up your time," said Sarah.

"Honestly, I'm glad for the company."

"How's it going? Being the new priest in town?"

"I can tell it's gonna be a hard slog winning over some of the congregation."

"It's a small town, small minds. But stick in there."

"Oh, I will."

They came out into a broad clearing. There was a lake in the middle and beyond the lake, at the top of a steep slope, was the forest. The wind had whipped up a little, sending ripples across the water.

"So what's causing you to doubt your sanity?" asked Devlin. "And why choose to come to me about it?"

"I'm going through a bit of an upheaval. Things I thought were set in stone turned out to be not stone at all, more like quicksand. I broke up with my fiancée a few weeks back and in the space of a few days, I lost my relationship and my home."

"That's tough. You have people around you to go to? For support?"

"I have friends and my mom. So I'm okay. It could be worse. But there have been moments I felt like I was losing my head a little."

"That's not so surprising with everything you're dealing with."

"Mmmm. See, it's more than just what's happened recently. All my life I've had a feeling that something's missing. Like there's a hole in me. When I had my relationship and my job, that was enough to distract me. Now I realize that was all they were. Distractions. And I wonder, does everybody feel like that? Do you feel like that?"

"I used to."

"What did you fill the hole with?"

"I guess I filled it with responsibility. Duty. A kind of heaviness."

"That doesn't sound like a very attractive solution."

Devlin chuckled. "No. No, you're right. But it's meaning, and I like it better than not having it. And meaning... It doesn't just present itself to you. You have to make it."

"Did you ever want children?"

For a split second, the image of his pregnant wife flashed before him and a chasm of grief threatened to open up in Devlin, a chasm he needed to look away from. So he lied. "No. That wasn't for me."

For a while they walked on in silence and Sarah seemed deep in thought.

"The emptiness I feel," said Sarah. "It's... real. There really is something missing." Sarah stopped suddenly and so did Devlin. "Father, there's something downright weird happening to me. It's so weird I'm afraid to tell anyone. But I have a feeling about you, that I can tell you."

"You're right. You can. I've seen plenty of 'weird,' so to speak."

"Okay, here goes. Recently I saw a medium, a mystic." Sarah paused. "Don't look at me like that, it was a one-off thing, a whim. I'd split up with my boyfriend of ten years. I was in crisis mode. Looking for meaning. Anyhow, it all went like you'd expect; the whole thing was a crock. Cold reading, fishing for reactions. However, right at the end, something weird did happen. Something that freaked her out as much as me. One by one the pictures on the wall of her cabin started to fall to the ground of their own accord. And she said something really strange, she said she could see another face in my face. She said it was like there was someone else hiding inside me. I don't mind admitting it left me shaken. Then I figured it was just a cruel trick, and that she was a hustler, a fraud. Taking advantage of vulnerable and gullible folk."

Devlin didn't answer. His mind had been cast back to their first meeting outside the church. The fast-moving shadows in the courtyard and the strange effect it seemed to have on Sarah's face. But it had been so brief and intangible Devlin had dismissed it as the workings of his imagination.

"Are you okay?" asked Sarah.

"Yes, yes. I was just thinking about what you've said."

The two stopped walking and stood by the banks of the lake.

"Well, here's where it takes a slightly stranger turn," Sarah continued. "I went back to the mystic." She reached inside her coat and took out a plastic folder. She took out the contents of the folder, about half a dozen sheets of paper, and handed them to Devlin.

"What's this?"

"Sketches of what the medium saw when she gave me a reading. Ever since I went to her cabin she's been obsessed with what she says she saw. She's been drawing and re-drawing the face she believes she saw. What the hell does it mean?"

Devlin sifted through the drawings, studying them intensely.

"What do you think?" asked Sarah.

"They're powerful sketches."

"Yeah, they are. But you know what I think? I don't think that's about talent. I think that's the power of the image she's seeing coming through. It's the drawing of someone who's really haunted by something. Amber Luna — that's the name of the medium. Well, it isn't really, obviously, it's Lucy. She said to me that she was a fake until she met me. And I believe that. And if I believe that, then I believe these images. Then, on top of that and everything, I've had the strangest dreams. Such strange dreams. It's like these weird dreams are starting to have more reality than... well, my reality."

Sarah looked at the ripples on the lake vanishing before they hit the shore and thought for a while.

"What do you think, Father?"

"I believe everything you say. Like I said, I've seen some strange things in my life, as extraordinary and other-worldly as the things you've experienced. I think everything you've said means something. Maybe we can work out what that meaning is."

As Sarah listened to Devlin's words she suddenly felt the most enormous lightness. As if a heaviness she had been carrying for years had lifted. They stood in silence for a while longer, the wind passing through the bare branches and over the lake. Then they pressed on, climbing a steep and uneven grassy slope that was difficult and tiring to navigate. Above them, they could see the hem of the forest, below them the town spread out in the bowl of the valley. They stopped for breath and took in the view.

"It's a tougher walk than it looks," said Sarah.

"Sure is. You said you've been having dreams. What kind of dreams?"

Sarah smiled, took a breath, and looked around her. "Dreams where I feel like I can't breathe and I'm falling."

"That does sound like classic anxiety."

"Yeah. But I always see the exact same thing and I can't figure out why. It feels like I'm drowning or going blind, and then I see forest and a night sky as if I'm looking at it over many months, the days and nights passing. And, at the end, always I see the same shape, always, like seven yellow snakes bound together." She threw up her hands. "Ah, I don't know why I'm asking you about dreams. I should see a shrink."

Sarah stopped talking. She was suddenly aware that Devlin was gazing across the river. That he was away in another world.

"Father? Father Devlin? You okay?"

Devlin didn't reply immediately, but when he finally turned toward her his eyes seemed to glitter.

"Seven yellow snakes?"

"Yeah..."

"Let me show you something."

"THAT'S IT. That's exactly what I saw in my dream. Exactly."

Devlin's flashlight was illuminating the vaulted ceiling of the old church crypt. They were standing by the shallow trench where the body, now excavated and taken away, had lain. Above them was the yellow painted symbol.

"It's the same color. The same weird way the snakes' bodies are tied together too. Is it a symbol? What does it mean?"

"See, I didn't think they were snakes till you told me about your dream. I thought it could be a tree. The tree of life."

"The one in the Garden of Eden?"

"Yes. But whatever it is, I think it's related to the body. The person who put the symbol there knows what happened to the body below."

"Who would have done it?"

"I don't know. There's not much I do know about this old ruin."

"Why's it still here?"

"A big family in the town have tombs here and have blocked selling the land off."

"Who?"

"The Driscolls."

"I know the name. They're local celebrities, kind of. Been in the town for four generations. Most people are happy to avoid them." Sarah gazed up at the ceiling. "Why am I seeing it in my dreams?"

Devlin arced his flashlight down into the shallow, empty trench where the skeleton had been.

"Is that where the body was?" asked Sarah.

"Yeah. The head was in the corner so it was laid out diagonally. Which is odd, the way the body was dug in at angles to the walls. At least I thought so."

"Can we go? It's horrible down here."

"Sure."

They turned to head out of the chamber with Devlin leading, but before he got to the stone arch he stopped and swung his torch back toward the empty trench.

"What? What is it?"

Devlin ran the torch up from the grave to the ceiling. "The painting. It's directly above the head of the grave."

DEVLIN AND SARAH sat on a low wall in front of the old church. From here they could make out the shapes of the old graveyard. Sarah shivered in her quilted winter jacket while Devlin pulled out a fresh Cohiba from his jacket. He paused for a moment and looked askance at Sarah.

"You don't mind?"

"I should... But I like the smell. My grandpa smoked cigars and pipes. And cigarettes come to that. He was a cloud with legs. How long have you smoked?"

"On and off since I was fourteen."

"You smoked those when you were fourteen?"

"No. I smoked Marlboro back then. I kicked the habit when I became a PJ."

"PJ?"

"Pararescue. I was a medevac in the Air Force. Had to kick the habit then or else I wouldn't have passed the first day of training. Then, when I became an investigator with the Air Force, I started up again. I went through cycles of giving up and starting back up. When I became a priest I moved on to these. I'm trying to cut down at the moment."

"Wow. All that suffering and reward. It's almost like a religion."

The wind was up again and the moon was rising. There was no cloud cover and the air was icy cold. But neither Devlin nor Sarah felt like going inside. Despite the weather, there was a comforting beauty about the night.

"So, what do you think?" asked Sarah. "About my dream? About what we saw?"

Devlin took the deepest drag his lungs could hold and then let it all drift out into the air. The satisfaction was immense. He studied the end of the cigar for a moment and thought.

"Dreams are impartial, spontaneous products of the unconscious psyche, outside the control of the will. They are pure nature; they show us the unvarnished, natural truth."

"What the hell does that mean?"

"It's a quote."

"It doesn't sound like the Bible."

"It's Carl Jung."

"What does it mean?"

"Dreams bring us back to ourselves. I think."

"But why did I see the symbol in the dream? The symbol in the crypt?"

"I don't know. There is something about that place, the body. Something that isn't at peace. Since I came to Avery it's been like I stepped through a looking glass."

"Is that Jung again?"

Devlin turned to Sarah. "I have a confession to make."

"That's weird. Shouldn't it be the other way around?"

"Normally, yes." Devlin took another hit and blew the smoke away from Sarah. "When I first met you, in the courtyard with the kids, I thought I was imagining it... But I..."

"What...?"

"I thought I saw, just for a moment, your face change."

"You mean like the psychic?"

"Yes, like the psychic."

"What did you see, exactly?"

"Your features grew darker. And your eyes, the color changed. But the sunlight was sharp and changing and I still now wonder if I wasn't imagining it. I certainly didn't think it was worth saying out loud. Then, when you told me what the psychic saw and then the sketches..."

"What the hell's going on? This is all kind of freaking me out."

They sat in silence for a while looking at the stars. Devlin smoked and seemed a thousand miles away. Completely lost in thought. Then he spoke again with a new intensity.

"What if the body has been returned from under the earth for a reason? Because, maybe, the time has come to unravel whatever put that poor soul there."

"And who's going to do that?"

"It's the cops' job. But I desperately want to know what happened to that boy. Your dreams, Sarah, they do mean something. They led you to the crypt and I think they may lead us to other places."

A shiver ran the length of Sarah's body. She folded her arms around herself and scanned the crooked outline of the old graveyard. "It's so weird this whole place still exists, don't you think? It's like the old creepy shadow of the new Holy Cross."

"Yeah. It is. Like I said, all I know is that the Driscolls have blocked any move to renovate the place. So they can protect their family plot."

"Where is their family plot?"

"Actually, I don't know."

"Well, why don't we go find it? For research."

Devlin smiled and shrugged. "Why not? Sounds like an interesting research project."

Treading carefully across the uneven ground and the broken stone, Devlin and Sarah examined the tombs one by one using Devlin's flashlight. Many of the engravings were faded but enough of the lettering had survived to identify them as not being a Driscoll tomb. It wasn't until they had reached the far corner of the cemetery that it became plain which of the plots must belong to the Driscolls. Standing taller by some way than any of the other headstones and monuments was a tomb as high and wide as a garage. It was made out of marble and overrun with creepers, though the outline of the building was still clear. Two Greek ionic columns stood on either side of a black wrought iron door consisting of two panels of intricate metalwork depicting angels. The columns supported a pediment which was inscribed with the name 'Driscoll.'

"Well, there's no doubt we're in the right place," said Sarah.

"They must have made a lot of money."

"But not all legally."

"How come?"

"The Driscoll family were bootleggers before the war. The first Driscoll came here in the twenties. They had links to the Gustin gang, a famous bootlegging outfit. Made a fortune out of smuggling booze over the Canadian border and into Boston."

"How do you know this?"

"From one of the kid's projects."

"I hope you gave him an A."

"Uh, no. It was Ash, one of the kids who broke in here. I kicked him off the project."

Devlin began inspecting the tomb, walking around it, and running his light over the stonework.

"It's in good shape."

"I guess they look after it."

"Yeah. It's in better shape than any of the other plots here." Devlin came back around the front of the tomb and suddenly stopped.

"What's up?"

"The stones here" — Devlin stamped on the ground — "sound like they're hollow."

"The tomb is probably underneath."

Devlin held the heavy padlock that secured the iron door in his hand and shone his flashlight on it. "This is a new lock. It's shiny and there are no marks."

"So?"

"So that's odd, a brand new lock in a derelict cemetery." Devlin suddenly raised his metal flashlight and brought the butt down on the lock.

"What the hell are you doing?"

"I keep hearing about Driscoll." Devlin brought the flashlight down on the lock again. "About how rich he is. How much money his family is worth." Now he was repeatedly hammering the lock against the lock as he spoke. "If they really valued this mausoleum they could move it lock, stock, and barrel over to the cemetery out front." The lock cracked and the shackle came free from the body. "I don't buy it and I don't buy that Driscoll's anything other than a low-life thug. I realize that's not a very

Christian thing to say of course. Especially since I officiated at his son's marriage."

Devlin had pushed the iron door open and was pointing his flashlight into the tomb. On either side, half a dozen coffins had been stacked in stone containers with name plaques on the side. Devlin pointed his flashlight at the floor, which was paved, except in the middle where there was a square manhole cover. The cover was gray and shiny and, like the lock, nowhere near the age of the rest of the tomb. He knelt and ran his fingers over the surface. In the middle of the cover was a handle. Devlin pulled at it and the cover came away. He aimed his flashlight down into the square hole.

"Stairs," said Devlin. "I can see metal stairs." Devlin began lowering himself down through the hole.

"What're you doing?"

"Research. I think I'm going to be one of your best students."

Devlin disappeared and Sarah peered down after him.

"What do you see?"

"Why don't you come down and look for yourself?"

Sarah glanced at the dark graveyard outside and the darker tomb around her. Then she shuffled her legs over the edge of the square hole and felt with her feet for the stairs. Despite the lack of light she made a smooth job of climbing down, joining Devlin who was already inspecting their surroundings with his flashlight. Lights suddenly flickered on.

"Whaddya know? There's a regular light switch down here. There must be a generator somewhere too," said Devlin who Sarah could now see standing by a light switch on the wall. She also saw that they were in a large room about twelve feet by twelve feet and hewn out of rock. There were empty metal shelves on three sides of the walls, and in the fourth wall was the arched entrance to a tunnel.

Devlin ran a fingertip over one of the shelves, licked it, and smacked his lips. "Coke."

"Should a priest know what cocaine tastes like?"

"No, but an Air Force detective should."

He pointed his flashlight at the tunnel entrance. "Let's go see where this leads."

"Do you think that's wise?"

"Just stick with me and you'll be okay."

"I hope you're right."

The tunnel led off in a straight line and, after what seemed to Sarah like an age, they found the end of it where a ladder led upwards. Devlin climbed and Sarah followed. At the top of the ladder was another square metal hatch. Devlin pushed against it, but it was locked from the other side. He braced himself and heaved his back and shoulder against the hatch. It gave a little, and dust and bits of dirt rained down into the shaft, covering him and Sarah. Then he rammed the hatch repeatedly until whatever was securing it on the other side began to give, and the hatch flew open revealing a clear night sky overhead.

Devlin and Sarah scrambled to the surface and looked around.

"Where the hell are we?" asked Sarah.

"In the middle of nowhere by the looks of things. Although..." Devlin listened intently for a moment. "I think I can hear traffic." He turned and squinted into the distance. "I think the turnpike must be not too far off. Conveniently, the turnpike goes to Boston."

"What does that mean?"

"I guess it means the Driscolls never really got out of the bootlegging business. Though it ain't gonna be liquor they're shipping."

16

Driscoll came to the station with his son. They hadn't been arrested or charged, and there was little likelihood they would be. But both had agreed to come in for questioning. Detective Hennessy had only wanted to pull Driscoll in, but the son insisted on accompanying his father to the station.

The two men were escorted down a hallway and caught sight of Devlin sitting by detective Hennessy's desk on the other side of the glass partition. Driscoll glared at Devlin but didn't stop.

"Thanks for coming in, Tony," said Hennessy, who had been sitting in the interview room waiting for Driscoll to arrive. A uniformed officer stood by the door.

Hennessy nodded at Driscoll's son. "Callum."

"Ted," Callum replied, before he and his father sat opposite Hennessy. Both looked about as pissed as he'd expected them to be.

"What's all this about, Ted?" asked Driscoll. "Will I need my lawyer?"

"You can call for your lawyer anytime you like. It's actually a sensitive matter I needed to talk to you about."

"Sensitive?"

"It's about the family tomb in the old church."

Callum shifted awkwardly in his chair. His father remained motionless and unimpressed.

"What about it?" asked Driscoll.

"We think it's being used to store illegal drugs. There's a room that's been carved out beneath it and a tunnel that runs from the tomb to a remote site south of the Massachusetts's turnpike.

"What? What the hell...?" said Callum looking suitably horrified.

"Someone's dealing drugs out of the family tomb?" asked Driscoll, looking as incensed as his son. "That's crazy. How has that been allowed to happen? Is anyone talking to the priest about this? Devlin? I saw him back there. He should be in here answering questions. This is a goddamn outrage..."

"It was Father Devlin who discovered the tomb had been tampered with. The place is covered with traces of powder that tested positive for cocaine and MDMA. Now obviously, the first thing I needed to do was make you aware, Tony, due to the upsetting nature of the discovery. I'm afraid I also need to ask you difficult questions..."

"Such as...?"

"When was the last time you or anyone you know visited the tomb?"

"We go twice a year, every year, to lay flowers on the anniversary of our parent's death. Father O'Neil always lets us in and accompanies us. Last time we went there was early September on the anniversary of my mother's death."

"And you didn't notice anything unusual?"

"Nothing."

"And that's the last time you were there?"

"I hope you're not implying anything here, Ted. That would be very unwise, in the circumstances."

Hennessy didn't answer. Instead, he glanced down at the sheets of paper in front of him and cleared his throat.

"So what're you gonna do about this, Ted?" asked Driscoll.

"We're gonna find who's responsible, Tony."

"What about the sacrilegious disturbance to my family's place of rest? What about that?"

"Restoring the tomb is something the church will need to talk to you about."

"Damn right, they will. I'll talk to that new priest myself. Stuck up son-of-a-bitch that he is. Is that it? Can we go now?"

Hennessy leaned back. "I just need to ask you one more thing."

Driscoll narrowed his eyes. "What?"

"Whoever was storing drugs in your family tomb might be linked to the body we found in the crypt."

"I heard that body was from about thirty years ago or more," said Callum.

"We're still working on the forensics to establish the exact circumstances of the death."

"What exactly are you asking me, Ted?" said Tony Driscoll, not bothering to disguise his simmering anger.

"It's no secret that a few of your cousins and nephews have records for dealing, Tony. Do you think any of them could be linked to the family tomb? Or the body we found?"

Callum had leaped to his feet and began yelling down at Hennessy. Such was his fury, that he might have jumped over the desk and gone for Hennessy had the officer not stepped forward and put a warning hand on his holstered pistol.

"You gutless son-of-a-bitch. How dare you?" Callum raged. "This is our family grave where my grandpa and grandma lay buried. How dare you insult us you fat, no good mother..."

"Sit down, Callum," said Driscoll calmly.

"What? Are you just gonna let this moron—?"

"Just sit down, son. The detective is doing his job like he has to."

"But... It's nothing to do with us. We don't even need to be here!" Callum turned back to Hennessy. "You need to talk to Father O'Neil... He's the one you need to talk to."

"Why?" asked Hennessy.

"Sit down, Callum," said Driscoll again, his voice raising. But Callum wasn't listening to his old man and continued his rant.

"He's the one been visiting the old church in the middle of the night... Bringing flowers... I've seen him wander up into the hills too in the early hours... Weird as hell if you ask me. Everyone's heard the rumors about him, and it don't take an idiot...."

"Shut up and sit the hell down..." barked Driscoll. "Now!"

Callum seemed to realize now that he'd said more than enough and sat glancing nervously over at his father.

"How do you know Father O'Neil visited the old church at night?" asked Hennessy.

Callum didn't answer right away. He was still breathing fast and trying to calm down. "I don't. I just heard rumors is all. Like everyone else."

"Those rumors are horseshit," stated Driscoll flatly. "I know everything there is to know in this town and I know that's downright horseshit."

"But you didn't know about the tomb being used for drugs?" asked Hennessy. "I mean to say, you know everything there is to know about this town, but you don't know about that?"

"Can we go, detective Hennessy?" said Driscoll. "Or is it time to call my lawyer?"

. . .

DEVLIN AND SARAH were still waiting when Hennessy got out of the interview room. He sat down at his desk and folded his arms.

"Well?" asked Sarah.

"Garbage. Everything they said. The whole operation is theirs, and they know it and I know it and they know I know it. But we don't have any evidence."

"What about fingerprints?" asked Devlin.

"We haven't found any yet. Not on the shelves or the entrances. They would've been careful I expect and used gloves. Driscoll is many things but he's about as far from an idiot as you can get. The son though, he's not so smart. He started running his mouth off until his old man shut him down."

"What did he say?"

"Oh, nothing worth repeating. Just a lot of hot air. I'm starting to like Driscoll or one of his brood for the body in the church."

Devlin shook his head. "No. I don't see it like that."

"How come?"

"They wouldn't bury the body so close to their operation. And strangulation isn't how dealers kill people. It's guns and sometimes knives. Added to that, I think the symbol in the ceiling of the old crypt is connected to the body. It's right above the grave, and it makes sense if there was a ceremonial aspect to the burial that the body would be buried where it is."

"Ceremonial? You think we should be looking for devil worshipers or something? No, no. I don't think that old graffiti has anything to do with this."

"Have you spoken to Father O'Neil about all of this? As part of the investigation?"

"Sure. I spoke to him, and the Bureau did too. He denies any knowledge of it. Says he never goes to the old crypt. And I've known Father O'Neil for thirty years. The man couldn't do something like this. Not morally and not physically. No, if it's anyone it's Driscoll. He's a rotten son-of-a-bitch and he's in the right place for it. Running an illegal operation out of the old church. As far as I'm concerned Driscoll is a prime suspect and that's what I'm telling the Bureau too. It certainly ain't anything to do with symbols and witchcraft or whatever."

17

"Hey, bro."

"Jamie? What...? What're you doing here...?"

"I come to see my bro, dude. Well, my half-bro."

"Did they let you out of the detention center?"

"No man, I got out of Worcester three months ago. I'm back at school."

"Who is it, Mikey?" A woman's voice came from inside the apartment but Mikey didn't answer. He was still looking in alarm at his half-brother standing in the hall.

"But... but... they just let you out?" stammered Mikey.

"Yeah, I got a few days to spend at home. Not that I'm saying this is my home, but for a few days... I thought it would be good to see you... and Julie... and my little nephew, for the first time of course."

"Who is it?" came the woman's voice again.

"Well, you can come in but..." Mikey scratched his head and looked uncomfortable. "It's tight for room here so you can't stay."

"Yeah, yeah. That's okay."

"Sure. Okay. Well, come in and say hello. You look like crap by the way."

"Been a long trip."

"When was the last time you had a shower?"

"Couple of days ago."

"Well, you stink. You can use our bathroom and you can wash and change your clothes while you're here too."

"Sure."

"Are you deaf? Who's at the door?" Mikey's wife, Julie, had appeared in the hall.

"Hi, Julie," said Jamie.

"Oh, Hi, Jamie. When did you get out of, uh...?" Julie said, tailing off, not exactly sure what the acceptable terminology for a detention center was.

"... the detention center? A few months back. I'm at a regular school now."

"Where do you live?"

"After I finished at the center they got me a placement in a children's care home."

"And you can just walk out when you like?"

"Yeah, of course, it's not a lockdown facility. I'm not Hannibal Lecter."

"But you're fifteen," said Mikey. "How can they just let you leave?"

"I gave them mom's address and that was fine."

"You're staying with mom?"

"I was going to but then I changed my mind. What with mom's situation and everything."

The three stood for a moment in silence, which was only broken by the cry of a baby.

"How's my nephew?" asked Jamie. "Can I see him?"

"Not right now," said Mikey. "We're just trying to get him down. Why don't you take a shower, buddy. The bathroom's at the end of the hall on the right."

"Great. It's a nice place you got."

"Yeah. We were on the list for affordable housing. Having a baby coming really sped things up."

With his backpack and sleeping bag hung on his shoulders, Jamie disappeared into the bathroom. Julie and Mikey went to see to their crying son in the main bedroom.

Mikey changed his son's diaper and handed him to Julie, who sat in a chair and breastfed him.

"Well that's a bolt out of the blue," said Julie in a hushed voice.

"I told him he can't stay."

"You what?"

"I said he couldn't stay."

"Are you kidding me? He's your brother."

"Half-brother. And I haven't seen him in over a year. Honest to God, if I had never heard from him again I wouldn't have given it a second thought."

"Mikey!"

"It's the truth. I hardly have anything to do with him."

"He's your brother and he has nowhere to go. It's freezing out there. You want him to die on the streets? In the cold? Where's he gonna go?"

Mikey had to admit he didn't have an answer to that. Their mom was in a bad way and Jamie's father, well, even when he got out of the correctional institution it was anyone's guess whether he'd clean himself up.

"Yeah, nowhere. The kid's got nowhere."

"You don't believe that story about the children's home? Letting him out?"

"Of course not. But we've got no room here. We're tripping up over each other as it is. We have a five-week-old baby, no sleep, and not much money."

"We're not turning him away. He can take the spare room. We'll think about what to do tomorrow but tonight he stays with us. I couldn't have him wandering around in the freezing winter by himself. I couldn't have that on my conscience, Mikey."

The baby had drifted back to sleep on Julie's breast and delicately she put him back in the crib. When the baby slept Mikey felt a whole lot better about the world. Julie sat back in the chair and Mikey smiled at her.

"I guess that's one of the reasons I got with you, Julie. You're a kind person."

"One of us has to be."

Jamie came out of the bathroom looking shiny and clean with wet spiky hair. He sat on the couch in the living room next to Mikey.

"I'll make up the spare room for you, okay?" Mikey said.

"Great. Thanks. I'll leave tomorrow, I only wanted to drop in and say hi."

"Jamie, you have nowhere to go. You stay here till you go back to the home. When is that exactly?"

"Oh... Err... Day after tomorrow. But listen, if things are too tight here I can try mom's. You don't have to put me up."

"Yeah I do, Jamie. You're fifteen and there's no one else. So, yeah. I do have to put you up."

Julie had come in and was standing in the doorway listening to the conversation.

"Mikey's right Jamie. We've got enough room to have you stay a night or two. Okay?"

"Okay. Thanks."

Julie sat in the armchair and they watched some crappy, easy TV for a while. When Mikey put ESPN on, Julie gave it up and went to bed, leaving the two brothers on the couch. Mikey got himself a beer and Jamie a glass of coke. They watched Sports Center with Scott Van Pelt for around half an hour without much conversation.

"Mikey," Jamie said in a way that made Mikey feel edgy, as if a difficult question might be coming. "Can I talk to you about something?"

Mikey looked at Jamie with bloodshot eyes. He was a new father, sleep-deprived and out-of-his-depth. Afraid of what the night might bring and the early start he had in the morning.

"I don't know, Jamie. It's kind of late and I'm bushed. Can it wait until tomorrow?"

"Yeah. Absolutely. It can wait until tomorrow."

"Good. I have to get some sleep. The baby woke up twice last night so I'm just praying tonight will be better." He snapped the TV off with the remote. "I'll make up the spare room for you. If you need the bathroom in the night don't flush, or it'll wake little Joe."

"Sure."

Mikey made up the bed in the spare bedroom and said goodnight to his half-brother. Then he got into bed as quietly as he could, careful not to wake his wife and son. Before he put his head down he unlocked his cell and googled 'Boston Child Services' phone number.

Devlin was up early to prepare for Mass. He'd finished his coffee and was about to make his way to the church when his cell buzzed and Cardinal Hermes's name flashed up on the screen.

"Hector?"

"Gabe. I know it's early, I just wanted to let you know that the Holy Cross accounts are a dead end. There's nothing there that definitely proves any irregularity."

"So there's nothing suspicious going on?"

"The investigating accountant says it's more than likely that money is being hidden. We just can't prove it one way or the other. The overall cash flow at Holy Cross has remained healthy and, like I said before, there's a steady income from local donors too. But the overheads have gradually grown by about fifteen or sixteen percent, which is significantly greater than the average in other churches. So, though we can't say for certain, there is a pattern in the books. A possible pattern of funds being over-allocated to hide it being siphoned off."

"For what?"

"I just don't know. There's been no money spent on restoring the church, or capital projects undertaken. It's not like Father O'Neil has a flamboyant lifestyle. If anything, he's extremely abstemious as well as being fiercely private."

"Do you want me to keep looking into this?"

"No. You've done a great job, Gabe. Exactly what I asked for. I'm grateful. But I'm pausing for now. I need to think about how else I can approach this because I'm not giving up."

AFTER THE CALL, Devlin sat for a while at the kitchen table watching the morning darkness begin to lift. He knew he'd have to visit Father O'Neil again to keep him up to speed with the police investigation and other more mundane church matters. The prospect gave him no pleasure.

Devlin dropped his mug in the sink and resisted the urge to smoke. As he made his way to the church he saw Susan Hennessy sitting in her car in the small parking lot. She was on her cell having an animated conversation and didn't see Devlin walk by. Her slight frame was bolt upright, her cheeks flushed and shoulders hunched. As he watched Susan it occurred to Devlin that for Father O'Neil to be able to screen himself off from the world, to keep his privacy so rock solid, he would need an ally. An ally who might do anything he asked.

DEVLIN HEADED to the sacristy in the back of the church and prepared himself for Mass. Once robed, he greeted the altar servers and went through the order of the morning's Mass.

Soon the church began to fill with worshipers, and once they had settled the Mass commenced. From behind the altar, Devlin greeted the faithful. As the reply, "And with your spirit," came back, Devlin noticed Susan Hennessy sitting pensively in an aisle seat.

Devlin had planned his homily that morning to be on courage. But suddenly, seeing Susan Hennessy sitting rigidly with her hands grasping her knees, he had an impulse to address her directly and began quoting Psalm 56.1.

"Behold, you delight in truth in the inward being, and you teach me wisdom in the secret heart."

As he spoke, he looked straight into Susan Hennessy's eyes.

"I think," said Devlin, addressing the congregation but with his eye on Susan Hennessy, "that Psalm 51.6 asks us to be true to ourselves if we are to be true to God. And that truth within ourselves will not be an easy truth, it will be a hard truth. In fact, often we will find it much easier to follow someone else's truth because it absolves us of our responsibility to ourselves, to that sacred part of ourselves that cannot be lied to. Our conscience. We cannot be servants to anyone else, man or God if we are not true to ourselves."

Devlin watched Susan Hennessy as she avoided his gaze. Instead, she stared down at her hands that were grasped tightly together.

After Mass had finished, Devlin mingled among the congregation then intercepted Susan on her way back to her car.

"Father." Susan gave Devlin a quick nod and began to walk away.

"Susan."

Susan stopped and turned back. "I'm really in such a hurry. What is it, Father?"

"Have you seen Father O'Neil lately?"

The question seemed to catch Susan off guard, and she hesitated before answering. "I'm actually seeing him now."

"I see. Susan, I know I'm only the fill-in here but I hope I would be able to count on you in the same way Father O'Neil did."

"Well, of course... Why would you think otherwise?"

"Because I think Father O'Neil might be a man who asks for a high level of loyalty from those he regards as especially close to him."

"We should all value loyalty, should we not? I don't know if I'm becoming paranoid, but I had the distinct feeling that your homily was aimed at me, Father."

"I hope it might strike a chord with all of my congregants. The message is universal, after all. To thine own self be true."

Susan pursed her lips, turned on her heels, and hurried to her car. Devlin watched her go, unable to shake the feeling that something was eating away at Susan Hennessy.

D evlin took a Bible class in the church hall and, after the class had dispersed, he loitered for a moment in front of the church. The sexton had closed the gates, and night had fallen. A flurry of snow that wasn't destined to settle drifted down. Devlin gave into the need for a smoke and lit up a cigar. He mulled over the extraordinary events with Sarah and the question hanging over Avery of who exactly had been murdered and buried in the old crypt. Though only a few of the parishioners had broached the subject with Devlin, he sensed it was in the front of their minds and on the tips of their tongues.

Devlin knew that it had happened again. As it was destined to happen. Like it happened in Sag Harbor, and in Halton Springs, and exactly as Lemus had prophesied. Wherever he went evil rose up to meet him.

Here, now, standing in the falling snow under the eaves of the church, he felt shadows creeping in around him. From the body being found to Sarah Wilson's strange experiences, he understood instinctively that something dark had lain dormant here in Avery for some time and that his presence was now stirring that darkness.

With a head light with nicotine and his mouth full of the tang of tobacco, Devlin made his way back to the rectory. When he reached the rectory door, he froze. The door was ajar, and scuffed and splintered where it had been forced open.

There were no lights on inside the house. Devlin threw his cigar to the ground, slipped in through the doorway, and stood motionless in the hall. A strip of moonlight from the door slanted across the wooden floor. It was deadly quiet until from upstairs Devlin heard a floorboard squeak. He crossed the hall and began to climb the stairs. Despite his best efforts to move quietly, the old floorboards gave little moans under the slightest pressure, so by the time Devlin had reached the landing he was pretty sure whoever had broken in knew they had company.

Upstairs only faint light from a large hall window gave minimal illumination. There were three rooms on the second floor; the bathroom, the guest bedroom, and the master bedroom, though only the door to the master bedroom was open. Keeping his movements as light as possible, Devlin sidled up beside the master bedroom door. It was so deathly quiet he could hear rhythmic breaths coming from whoever was in the room. Quick breaths that betrayed a rising panic.

Devlin reached a hand around, feeling for the switch, and flicked it on. As soon as the room lit up the intruder came charging out wielding a tire iron. Devlin ducked the length of iron as it came whistling toward him and missed the chance to block the intruder who had already reached the top of the stairs. There was enough light for Devlin to make out a well-set man of average height wearing a balaclava.

The guy in the balaclava stumbled down the stairs and Devlin flew after him, through the hall and out into the freezing air. Like the night before, the intruder headed diagonally across the cemetery in the direction of the road. But this time Devlin was close behind and the chances of the other guy making it to the road were diminishing. As Devlin caught up, making his larger strides count, his target suddenly turned and came flying at him with the tire iron. Devlin took a dive and felt the whoosh of the iron only inches away. The momentum of the tire iron took its owner off balance. Sensing the narrowest of openings Devlin launched himself at his opponent, forcing him down onto the soft, wet ground where Devlin could use his superior weight and strength to pin him to the floor. In one movement he grasped the shaft of the tire iron, ripped it out of the attacker's hand, and threw it into the air, where it ricocheted off a head-stone before landing on the grass. Then Devlin planted a series of fists into the face of the man squirming beneath him until he stopped squirming.

Finally, Devlin had a moment to take stock and catch his breath. He sat back on his heels and took a good look at the figure on the ground. With both hands, he rolled the balaclava back and realized that he recognized the face beneath it.

DEVLIN PULLED up a wooden chair by the couch, where the unconscious intruder lay prone, and waited. After a few minutes, the man on the couch started to moan as he came to, clutching his face.

Devlin went to the kitchen and came back with a glass of water and two pills.

"Here, you'll need this."

The man got himself up on his elbows, and managed to swing his legs so he was sitting up. Then he took the glass and gulped back the pills.

"Son-of-a-bitch..." he muttered. "You got a hell of a slug for a priest." He looked up at Devlin with heavy, bloodshot eyes. He had a neatly trimmed black beard, but his black hair was flat and messy, plastered over his head from the balaclava.

"It's Adam, isn't it?" asked Devlin, who had the man's wallet open in his hands. "Adam Berry. I met you in Avery the other day. Outside the coffee shop. Susan Hennessy introduced us."

"Yeah..." He nodded slowly, eyeing his wallet and ID card sourly. "How long till they get here?"

"You mean the cops...?"

"No, I mean the cast of Miss Saigon. Of course, the cops."

"Depends."

Berry looked confused. "You haven't called them?"

"Not yet. And if you tell me why a man who sits on the Education Board is breaking into a rectory, maybe I won't."

"What if I'd rather you call the cops?"

"You and I know, with a criminal record for breaking and entering, you'd lose your job. And then there'd be the gossip. Why someone like you was burgling a place like this."

Berry didn't answer. He put his glass down on the floor and eyed the door.

"I wouldn't try it," said Devlin. "If you move so much as an inch from that couch I'll lay you out all over again."

"Christ. What kind of priest are you?"

"The kind that served in the Air Force. The kind that's seen action. The kind that means business and wouldn't mind taking another shot at the guy that just tried to break his head open with a crowbar. And by the way, I'd make sure that was on your rap sheet as well as the B & E."

Berry eyed Devlin warily as if seeing him for the first time, and getting a realistic picture of what he was dealing with.

He sighed. "Damn... What do you want to know?"

"More than I know already, which is that this isn't something you've done before."

"How would you know that?"

"You think experienced burglars take their ID with them when they go out on business?"

"No..." Berry hissed through his teeth.

"I want to know what it is you're looking for. And if you tell me, then, depending on what it is, I won't tell anyone else and certainly not the cops."

Berry rolled his eyes and rubbed his face, then sighed again, the biggest one so far. "You were in the Air Force?"

"Yeah."

"Where did you serve?"

"Afghanistan mostly. An FOB in the Ghazni province."

"Arian?"

"Yeah. Arian."

"I served too, in the army. Private First Class. Only did six months. My unit got attacked and I got hit with shrapnel. That and other things got me a medical discharge."

"Other things?"

"Irritable heart. That's what they called it in the Civil War. Now we call it PTSD."

"How are you now?"

"Well, you wouldn't believe it, but I'm getting better. What did you serve as?"

"Pararescue and then Air Force investigations."

"A PJ? Toughest training in the military they say."

"Marines would disagree."

Another flurry of snow came down outside.

"So tell me. What's going on, Adam?"

Berry rubbed his face. "Man alive. Ain't that a question?" Then he raised his head wearily and looked at Devlin. Berry was a handsome man, thick-set, carrying a little extra weight but otherwise looked as if he took care of himself. His hair and beard appeared to be dyed black and there was a heavy smell of aftershave coming off of him.

"It's a total SNAFU, Father. The whole thing."

"Tell me. You never know, I might be able to help."

"Well, I guess the place to start is simple enough. I'm being blackmailed."

"By who?"

"Father O'Neil."

"What's he got on you?"

Berry leaned back and shrugged. "I'm a married man, Father. But I guess I'm just not as good at being a married man as I should be. You know what I mean?"

"I'd rather you tell me what you mean."

Berry threw up his hands. "I have a restless nature. A roving eye... I'm a hard dog to keep on the porch..."

"You're unfaithful to your wife."

"Yes..."

"More than once."

"I know... I know that's bad. I know I should have some self-control. But honestly... I don't know how other men do it. And me and Annie... That's my wife... It hasn't been easy. She... She lost interest in that side of things."

"I'm not here to give you spiritual counseling or marriage counseling. How other men keep faithful to their wives or they to their husbands is no mystery. You don't get born faithful. It's a choice you make and you stick by it or you don't."

"Takes all sorts to make a world, Father. We ain't all of us saints. Some of us just have to live with our flaws."

"And that's working out real well for you. Burgling houses, swinging tire irons around, and being knocked on your ass in the middle of the night. But I guess that's just how it is when you live with your flaws. What evidence?"

"Huh?"

"You said Father O'Neil had evidence. What evidence?"

"Letters. I had... a thing with a woman who went to Holy Cross. It wasn't just a one-night thing. I was crazy over her as a matter of fact. She worked in the same building as me and I used to drop her little love notes. Put them in her desk drawer. I knew it was risky but I was in love with her. At one point I even wanted her to leave her husband for me. Well, long story short, she didn't. She was just so wrecked with guilt about it all that she called it off and stayed with her husband. I was heartbroken. And if that wasn't bad enough, she went and confessed to O'Neil. And she got it into her head that if she wanted forgiveness from God, penance, she should hand over my notes to O'Neil too. To get rid of her shame and sin."

"So, O'Neil has your love notes and that's what you were looking for?"

"Yeah."

"How many times did you try to get into the rectory?"

"Half a dozen. I'd watched O'Neil for a while. He was out of the rectory more than he was in, and I saw he had a habit of heading out for a walk around eleven or midnight most nights. So I'd watch him go, see him head out, and then I'd go for it."

"Where did he walk to?"

"Up to the woods on the other side of the cemetery. Over beyond the turnpike and past the lake."

"Was he heading anywhere specific?"

"Seemed to me he was heading for Oak Ridge, the forest just north of Holy Cross. But to be honest I was too busy trying to get into the rectory."

"How long was he gone for on these walks?"

"Couple of hours or more. Thing is, even though Father O'Neil was nowhere around, I still had the sexton prowling the grounds. So I didn't have much time anyway before I saw the sexton's flashlight and had to skedaddle. Upshot was I spent hours sitting in the car waiting for a window between O'Neil out walking and Joe, the sexton before the new guy came, patrolling."

"Didn't you think that was odd? Father O'Neil, a frail, seriously ill man in his sixties was walking up steep slopes to a forest in November at midnight? And he was doing this most nights?"

"Yeah. Now you say it to me like that, I guess it is. And if I didn't have other personal priorities at the time I would have wondered about it more myself."

"You said he was blackmailing you. What did Father O'Neil want from you?"

Berry shifted on the couch and rubbed his knees. "He... He asked me to let him know the schedule for approval for private schools in the Greater Boston area. I have access to that 'cos I'm the Schools Superintendent."

"He didn't want money?"

"Nope."

"It's kind of a specific thing to be blackmailed about."

Berry shrugged. "Maybe, maybe not. It's valuable information to some people. I guess he wanted it so he could give the local Catholic schools a heads up about scheduled re-approvals. After they get an initial approval when they first set up we review them periodically. Our reports can make or break a school."

"Did you give him the schedule?"

"No. Not yet. But I have it hanging over my head now. The whole time. It's all I think about. If O'Neil comes through with his threat, I could lose it all, my marriage, my job..."

"And you won't go to the police because of who Susan Hennessy's husband is?"

"No. I damn well won't. Jeez, the three of them are thick as thieves anyway. It wouldn't surprise me if they were all in on it, blackmailing me. They're like an unholy trinity. I don't know which one of them's the worst. Although if you believe the rumors it's O'Neil."

"What rumors?"

"The usual. He has a thing for boys."

"Has anyone made a complaint against him?"

"Not that I know of."

"So who told you about it?"

"It's what people say. Give me a break. Like I said, it's a rumor. Might be nothing in it."

Devlin didn't say anything. He just gazed at the floor for a while, deep in thought. Finally, Berry could stand the silence no longer.

"What is it? What are you thinking?"

"It's just an odd thing to blackmail someone for. A schedule for school reapprovals?"

"I guess. But then I figured that was the first thing. Then it would be something else, something bigger maybe. He'd always have me in his thrall. Unless I got the notes back." Berry glanced up to the ceiling, toward O'Neil's bedroom and office.

"He took all his belongings with him to his sisters," said Devlin. "I doubt he'd leave the letters here."

Berry slumped. "I guess. What the hell am I going to do?"

"I can talk to Father O'Neil."

"Would you do that?"

"There's no reason why I should. You're a weak, vain, self-absorbed man who's reaping what he's sown. But what Father O'Neil's done isn't right. It isn't right at all."

Berry left and Devlin went outside for a smoke. Devlin reached into his pocket for his cigar and lighter, and felt a small round object hiding in the corner of the pocket lining. He took it out and realized it was the chestnut he'd found in the study on the day of Callum Driscoll's wedding. He read the Latin inscription again: 'I love you, forgive me.' Then he looked out over the lake and up at the forest that stretched over the hills to the north of Avery and Holy Cross. Late at night, it would be a strangely inhospitable walk, and physically nearly impossible for a man in O'Neil's state. He wondered what was driving O'Neil out there every night. What kind of demon? And what he might be looking for out there.

20

The next free space in Devlin's calendar was midday and he calculated he had enough time to fit in a trip to see Father O'Neil. This time he wouldn't ring ahead. He was outside the rectory and about to get into his car when someone called to him. He looked over toward the cemetery and saw Sarah at the head of a group of students.

"Morning," said Devlin as he approached the group.

"Hi," replied Sarah. "Is it okay if they continue with their research project today?"

"Of course. Be my guest."

Sarah told the kids to carry on and they headed off into the cemetery, clipboards and cell phones in hand.

"I told them they had to behave themselves or I'd bring down holy hell on their heads. No disrespect intended."

"None taken. I meant to call..." Devlin paused, his attention caught by a car that had come in from the road. It pulled up just short of Devlin, and Sarah and Detective Hennessy got out.

"Father, Sarah," said Hennessy.

"Detective," replied Devlin.

"I came because I have some news on the body..." But

Hennessy didn't get any further. Sarah suddenly interrupted, her eyes wide with a sudden realization that seemed to come from somewhere deep inside of her.

"It's to do with me..." she said with starling conviction. "The boy who was murdered... He's connected to me... Isn't he...?"

"Well, yes... But, uh, how...?" Hennessy stuttered. Then he recovered his composure, and his tone and expression became softer, more sympathetic. "Sarah, I have to tell you something that will come as shock. The DNA on the crypt body came back with a match on CODIS, and it matched you, Sarah. We had your details on file from a drugs raid in Boston."

Sarah shook her head. "Right. My slime ball ex, back before Tom, was small-time dealing without me knowing. The cops swabbed me during the raid."

"The lab results match your DNA, Sarah. The forensic report says he's a close relative of yours... That you shared a parent. He was your half-brother, Sarah. I went by the school first and they said you'd be here... But how did you know I was here about you?"

Sarah didn't answer. She was deep in thought. For a moment the only sound was the chatter and laughter coming from the students.

"Did you know you had a younger half-brother, Sarah?" asked Hennessy.

"No, I didn't and it doesn't make any sense..." Sarah felt dizzy with confusion and Hennessy's words echoed around her head. A younger half-brother? How could that be? How could she have a younger brother she didn't know about? It made no sense at all. Her mind raced to find the answer and, in a moment of pure revelation, the answer hit her with the force of a punch in the stomach. Her body trembled, and all the little things that had never added up suddenly added up. *Of course that's the answer*, she thought as she ran back over her life and how she had never quite felt like she fitted in. How could it ever have been any other way?

"I need to round up my class and get them back to school. And then we need to go have a talk with my mom. A long-overdue talk. About secrets."

21

"Sarah?"

"Hi, Mom,"

For a moment Sarah's mom couldn't put it together. Standing on her porch with her daughter were two men, Detective Hennessy, and a tall priest she didn't know. Her mind started to reel and she feared the worst.

"Dear God, what on earth has happened? Is it Theresa...?"

"No. It's not Theresa. Nobody's been hurt. We just need to talk."

"What about?"

"About where I come from."

The color drained from Sarah's mother's face and for a moment Sarah thought she might faint. But then, very calmly and with an air of resignation, she replied, "Yes, of course. Please, come in."

Though the day was cold there was little cloud and the sunroom at the back of the house had warmed up. They all sat in wicker chairs set around a bare glass coffee table.

"Ted," said Sarah's mom, putting on a brave face.

"Mrs. Wilson," replied Hennessy.

She turned to Devlin. "I don't believe we've met?"

"Father Devlin. I'm the priest at Holy Cross."

"Ah. We're Methodist, Father. I go every Sunday."

"Ted and Father Devlin are here because..." Sarah began. "Well, because of why I'm here." Sarah spent a moment trying to line up her thoughts before she spoke. But her mom spoke first.

"How did you find out?"

"Not the way I should have," replied Sarah.

"I'm so sorry." And it seemed to Sarah that her mom was sorry. Tears had formed in her eyes.

"Not as sorry as me, Mom. Why didn't you tell me? Dear God, Mom, why? Only last week you were telling me off for not telling you about Tom. For keeping secrets. And all the time you were lecturing me, you... You were hiding the fact that I was adopted? Jesus, Mom..."

"I just... I always meant to, I swear to you... I'm so sorry, Sarah... Your father always told me we should tell you. He'd get very angry with me and I always said we should just wait a little longer. And I would have done. I would've told you. I swear. But when your father died so suddenly it changed everything. It was so awful." Tears dropped onto her cheeks. "I was devastated. I'd lost him forever... and I... I just didn't want to risk losing you too. Please, forgive me..."

"At least I know now why I never really looked like Theresa. Or you. I think I always knew. At some level, I always knew. I should've worked it out long ago. That's the piece of me I always felt was missing. But now I know what that missing piece is... The one way you can help me, Mom, the only way, is just to tell me the truth."

"The truth... Yes. I'll tell you the truth." She wiped her cheeks and cleared her throat. "After my hysterectomy, I still wanted another child. I don't think having an only child is a good thing. I suppose people would tell me I shouldn't say that. But then I'd point them to my cousin Allan, who is a strange soul. Very odd altogether. And we wanted to fill our house, your father and I. We went through an adoption agency and they had a baby whose mother couldn't look after her. The father wasn't around and she... Well, she just wasn't capable of looking after you. I don't know everything about her circumstances but I do know she had a drug problem. So we adopted you, Sarah."

"Where is she? My birth mother?"

"They lived in Florida but... Some years after I adopted you I was told your birth mother had died from a drug overdose. Please forgive me, Sarah... Please..."

"My birth mother is dead?"

"I didn't want to lie to you," she pleaded. "I didn't think it was a lie. I was protecting you..."

"From what?"

"From feeling like you'd been abandoned, rejected, were unloved."

Sarah tried to take it all in. "My birth mother is dead...? My birth mother's dead as well...?"

Sarah's mother shook her head in confusion. "... As well as who...?"

"I had a brother, Mom. A half-brother. But he's dead... Murdered..."

"What...?"

"That's why Ted and Father Devlin are here." Sarah felt herself choking up. She looked over at Detective Hennessy for support, who shifted in his chair, overheating in the bulky flight jacket he hadn't taken off.

"Recently," began Hennessy taking his cue, "a body was discovered in the grounds of Father Devlin's church." Sarah's mom looked over at Devlin. "We believe it was a homicide and the victim was buried there about fifteen years ago. A DNA test has matched the body as a close relative to Sarah. It's near to certain he was her brother."

Sarah's mom seemed to freeze and for a moment Sarah wondered if she was breathing.

"Mom...?"

"Oh... Dear"..."

Sarah leaned forward and clasped her arm, and found herself consoling her mother. "It's okay, Mom."

"We need to know as much as possible about Sarah's biological family, Mrs. Wilson," said Hennessy. "It's the only link we have to the body we've found."

Sarah's mother nodded solemnly. "I'm so sorry, Sarah."

Sarah heard herself replying, "I know."

"Do you have the name of the adoption agency?" asked Hennessy.

"Yes... I do. Somewhere. I think it's in a box with my late husband's things. I'll go and get it."

Mrs. Wilson left and after a few minutes returned with a large, worn envelope filled with papers, which she handed to Hennessy.

"Thank you, Mrs. Wilson. You've been a huge help, and I appreciate it."

The three guests rose and both Hennessy and Devlin left. Sarah remained and there was an awkward silence between mother and daughter.

"I hope you understand, Sarah."

Sarah nodded and put her hand on her mother's hand. But really, she didn't understand at all and then she remembered Tom's parting words to her; 'The one thing you lack, is the capacity to forgive.'

22

Jamie hadn't unpacked. He just wasn't comfortable there. What with the frosty reception he'd got, his nephew crying all the time, and Julie hardly talking to him, it was clear staying at his brother's apartment was not a sustainable situation. But where he went next was a mystery. He had no plan but to keep running, and what kind of plan was that? He was only fifteen and that meant there'd be a lot of running ahead of him. He didn't even want to think about the guy he'd hit with a brick. He'd kept replaying the moment in his head, trying to convince himself that the guy had survived. Someone once told him that there was a lot of blood supply to the head and that could explain how much blood there was. It was, he thought, possible the guy had survived. And with the miracles they can perform with modern medicine today, who knows? The more Jamie thought about it the more he got around to persuading himself he might not be a killer.

He was sitting on his bed playing Minecraft on his cell phone. He could play it for hours on end, whole days if nothing else got in his way. He'd started building a village for himself after lunch and was now filling the grounds with livestock. He'd hardly noticed night fall outside and the room become dark, other than the glow of his cell's screen. He'd even managed to screen out the periodic cries of the nephew and the mini-fights between Mikey and Julie. He'd managed to tune out from the rest of the world.

So, it was only gradually that his ears tuned in again to a new noise from another part of the apartment. It was the sound of two men talking very reasonably and occasionally laughing together. He turned his cell off and sat in the dark, listening intently. The first voice was his brother. He was talking in the hall. The other voice was deeper and more sonorous.

A cold shudder went through Jamie's body. He realized that he knew the new voice. It was the voice he'd been running from. *That son-of-a-bitch Mikey must have made a call,* he thought.

Jamie sat up in one jerky movement and slid his phone into his pocket. The voices were coming along the hall toward his room, so he slipped down underneath the bed where he froze, waiting.

There was a knock at the door. He heard his brother call his name. Then silence. His heartbeat sounded so loud, as did his breaths. How could they not hear him even on the other side of the door?

The handle turned and the door opened slowly. A line of light from the hallway appeared along the carpet. Then Mikey hit the switch and the whole room lit up.

"Jamie...?" said Mikey. "Weird. I thought he was here. Hey, Julie. Did you see Jamie go out?"

"I don't know. Maybe." Julie's voice was further away, disinterested, annoyed even.

"Maybe you'd like to wait?" Mikey asked the visitor. "There's his bag, so he definitely hasn't gone anywhere far. He's probably just gone down to the 7-Eleven on the corner. He won't be long."

"Sure," said the visitor. "Not a problem."

The light went off and the door closed. Jamie didn't move for a couple of minutes, fearing it was a trick, fearing that as soon as he got out from under the bed they'd come back in, grab him, and bundle him out.

So he waited it out, and by the time he did come out from under the bed he knew what he had to do.

He put on his coat, grabbed his backpack, and hooked it over his shoulders.

His room had a small balcony. The door to the balcony was always unlocked; Mikey used it to have a secret cigarette whenever he could get a minute away from his screaming son and the wife.

Jamie eased the door open, slipped out onto the balcony, and looked down. His brother's apartment was two stories up. Not as low as he'd like, but not so high as to make escape impossible. He straddled the metal railings and then pulled his other leg over. He crouched and, holding onto the bottom of the metal railings, he dropped down and for a moment he swung back and forth, then he held his breath and let go.

The moment he hit the ground he felt a sharp pain burning in his ankle. He toppled onto the cold, wet grass clutching his throbbing lower leg, cursing silently to himself. He lay still for a little while and at last the pain became a little less urgent. He managed to get to his feet and hopped into the night, alone in the world again and running away from a waking nightmare.

23

Through the frosted panes of glass Devlin watched the silhouette shuffle along the hallway. The door opened and Father O'Neil's drawn, sallow face glared up at Devlin.

"This is unexpected."

"I meant to ring ahead, but in the rush over here it slipped my mind."

O'Neil frowned. "Why did you need to 'rush' over here?"

"There are a few matters I need to keep you in the loop about. After all, I am only the 'fill-in' priest."

For a moment the two men stood looking at each other across the threshold

"Come in," said O'Neil, who began shuffling back toward the living room. Devlin followed. O'Neil sat in his armchair and Devlin took the couch.

"Well?" prompted O'Neil.

"The first thing I need to talk to you about is quite a sensitive matter."

O'Neil's face screwed up. "Sensitive? How?"

"It's about Adam Berry."

"What about him?"

"He accused you of blackmailing him. With letters he exchanged with a woman he was having an affair with."

O'Neil almost smiled. "And you believe him?"

"I hardly know him. Which is why I'm asking you."

"He's lying. Adam Berry is an appalling man who only thinks about one thing. God help his poor wife. I wouldn't trust anything that man said. He's vain, foolhardy, unrepentantly unfaithful, and completely lacking in morals and judgment. How he ever achieved superintendent is a mystery to all men."

"So you don't have the letters?"

O'Neil fixed Devlin a resentful stare. "Yes. I have them. The woman in question was tormented with regret. Utterly miserable and, as part of her lengthy confession, she felt compelled to give them to me. That it would ease her of her shame. I accepted for her good. But I most certainly wouldn't have used them for blackmail."

"Have you still got the letters?"

"Yes."

"Where are they?"

"I have them in my personal possession. They are, after all, deeply sensitive."

"Why haven't you destroyed them?"

"I meant to. I hadn't gotten round to it. You might have noticed I have other things on my mind at the moment. Is that all? Or have you just come to torment me over a faithless husband's love notes?"

Devlin didn't reply and O'Neil gave a bitter smile. "I thought so. Father Devlin, I have come to believe that you're a man who looks for injustice for his egotistical satisfaction. Driven by a mixture of narcissism and who knows what demons, you unravel other people's lives for your own strange pleasure."

"Why did you walk up to Oak Ridge in the middle of the

night?" O'Neil's smile vanished. "Berry said he saw you regularly walk out in the middle of the night up to the woods."

"I went for evening strolls. What the hell business is it of anyone but mine?"

"At midnight?"

"It wasn't that late."

"Berry says it was."

"You're taking Berry's word over mine? How would he know anyway?" O'Neil leaned forward. "Was he spying on me?"

"He was looking for an opportunity to get the letters back."

O'Neil clapped the arms of his chair. "Oh, this is too much. This is almost comical. You're interrogating me on the word of a man who cheats and spies? Why would I go up to Oak Ridge at midnight?"

"So no one would see you go."

"Oh, dear, Father Devlin. Yet again you see suspicion in the utterly mundane. I went for an evening stroll and certainly didn't get as far as Oak Ridge. I don't drive so I often go out by myself for walks."

Devlin nodded. "Oh, by the way," — he put his hand in his pocket and took out a small object — "I was in the study and found something you left behind. It was in a desk drawer." He held the chestnut up.

O'Neil began to twitch nervously. "Why have you brought that with you? It's just an old chestnut I picked it up on my walks."

"Did you inscribe it?"

"What?"

"The words, '*ambo te ignosce me,*' 'I love you, forgive me.' What do they mean?"

"It's just a chestnut. I don't remember why I doodled on it..."

"I thought it might mean something to you."

O'Neil paused, seemingly holding back from speaking. Then he said blankly, "No. It means nothing to me."

"Fair enough." Devlin repocketed the chestnut. O'Neil eyed him warily.

Devlin studied O'Neil for a moment as if trying to work him out, to see into him. "What is it, Father O'Neil?"

"What is what for heaven's sake?"

"The secret you're carrying?"

"If you're insinuating I had something to do with the body found in the old crypt, then may your soul rot in eternal hell. Now go!" O'Neil yelled. "Just leave me alone. It's late and..."

O'Neil suddenly looked panicked and glanced up at the clock on the wall. "Oh Lord, I have to take my meds." He reached for a pill organizer on the coffee table beside him, a plastic case with colored boxes labeled with the days of the week. He picked out the box for Monday and moaned in frustration. "Oh, for God's sake... I've left my painkillers upstairs in the bathroom."

"I can get them."

"No. I can do it..." O'Neil struggled to get up, collapsed back down, and gave up. "They're in the bathroom. In the cabinet above the sink. The label says 'Anexsia.' Get them and then leave me in peace, you awful man."

Devlin went upstairs to the bathroom and took the pills from the medicine cabinet. As he came out of the bathroom, he noticed that one of the doors along the landing was hung with a crucifix. Downstairs he could hear O'Neil coughing and cursing to himself.

Back in the living room, Devlin handed O'Neil the pills, who washed them down with a tumbler of water. He placed the empty tumbler on the coffee table and coughed hard.

"I'll get you some more water."

"Yes..." gasped O'Neil.

Devlin filled the glass in the kitchen but when he returned

O'Neil had fallen asleep. His head had lolled to one side against the armchair's headrest, and he was breathing deeply and rhythmically. For a moment Devlin watched O'Neil. He remembered Adam Berry's talk of rumors about O'Neil and he wondered if it could be true. O'Neil seemed to be dreaming; he moaned gently and his breathing became irregular. His body twisted a little in the armchair and his fingers twitched. Then his breathing returned to a steady rhythm and whatever had troubled his sleep went away.

Devlin headed for the front door, but halfway along the hall he stopped and looked back up the stairs. Instead of leaving, he climbed the stairs again and opened the door with the crucifix. From the shoes placed on the floor and the breviary and rosary on the nightstand, Devlin knew instantly it must be O'Neil's bedroom. Devlin paused over the nightstand and inspected the objects laid out on it. By the breviary was a 'spugna,' a round cork mat with pins sticking out that was used to self-inflict pain and repent sin. *As if O'Neil hasn't enough pain to endure in his life,* thought Devlin.

There was little else in the room that belonged to O'Neil. It was a sparse and clearly very temporary abode. Moving quickly and lightly, Devlin opened up the closet and rooted around inside. Then he opened the nightstand drawer, which was empty. Sitting on the bed, looking around the room for any other place that might be worth searching, his heel touched against something solid. He dropped down to his hands and knees and found a black brief case with a four-dial combination lock, which he pulled out.

Sitting back on the bed, Devlin placed the case on his knees with the locks facing him. It was, thought Devlin, a woeful kind of security, exactly the kind of security a sixty-five-year-old priest would use. He placed a thumb on the button beside one of the latches and scrolled through the first dial until he felt the lock give, then he repeated the process with the other three dials until the latch sprung open. Then he used the same four numbers, 1-9-5-7 — the year of O'Neil's birth, Devlin realized — to release the latch on the other side and opened the brief case up.

Inside the case were old letters in faded envelopes, and photographs of friends and relations. Sitting on top was a bunch of more recent letters held together with a bulldog clip. A cursory read of the top letter told Devlin enough to know what they were. He took them out and slipped them into this jacket pocket. Then he closed the case and put it back under the bed.

On the way out Devlin checked the living room. O'Neil was still asleep but moaning gently, his lips parted slightly and his thin fists clenched. Devlin headed out the front door leaving O'Neil to his tormenting dreams.

The sound of the door closing awoke Father O'Neil. As he came around he remembered his conversation with Devlin, and his face creased with pain and remorse. He heard a sudden howl and realized it was coming from within him. A great well of regret, guilt, and pain, built up over decades, had exploded from somewhere inside him and his forlorn wailing filled the room. Tears spilled down his face.

Eventually, the outburst subsided and he dried his eyes and face. Then he reached for his cell phone and dialed.

The person on the other end picked up.

"Hello," said O'Neil. The person on the other end of the line said something which angered O'Neil. "No, I'm not okay. I'm not okay at all!" He spat the words into the cell. "I am terrified. Terrified for my soul and body. That dreadful man Devlin was here again. I think he knows something. He's tormenting me. Torturing me. He won't let me be and I desperately need to be at peace with my Lord. I need to talk... Now..."

24

The knock was hard and insistent. *It can't have been the first knock,* thought Berry. He had come to in his armchair in his study. After a long day and a late meeting, a Chinese takeaway and half a bottle of wine had sent him plummeting into a deep sleep. Now his body complained as he pulled himself to his feet and walked stiffly to the door. Out in the hallway, he realized the house had become dark and silent. His wife and kids must have left for hockey practice while he was asleep. He hit the switch and the hallway lit up.

The knock came again. Harder and even more insistent.

"Okay, okay... For Christ's sake."

Berry opened the door and saw a large, broad figure throwing the porch into shadow.

"Father Devlin..."

"Can I come in?"

"What's it about?"

"I think you know."

Berry nodded and led Devlin down the hall, through the living room, and into his study. It was private here even if the wife and kids came back. He cleared books, papers, and his jacket off the two-seater couch and indicated to Devlin to take a seat. Devlin sat and Berry lowered himself into his armchair.

"What can I do for you, Father?"

"You don't have to worry about the letters Father O'Neil had."

Berry leaned forward in his chair, his sleepy eyes suddenly wide. "Do you have them?"

"I destroyed them."

"How did you...?"

"It doesn't matter."

"I don't know what... Thank you... Thank you... Jesus..." Berry took a quick breath in and swallowed, then clasped his forehead and for a moment he didn't move. Then he coughed, swallowed again, and filled his wine glass that had been sitting on the table by his elbow.

"How can I repay you?"

"You can come to confession."

"Confession? That it?"

"I think it's a start. Don't you?"

Berry nodded. "Of course." Then he gave a short laugh. "What will my penance be?"

"Long. And of course, I'll have a favor I can call in with you. Should I need it."

"Yeah, agreed." He raised his glass and took a sip of wine. "Sorry, that's rude of me. Do you want a drink?"

"No. But I do want to ask you some questions."

"What about?"

"Avery. You've been here a long time?"

"I have."

"I take it you heard about the body found in the old crypt?"

"'Course..."

"What's strange to me is that no one seems to know about any boy going missing here."

"It's a mystery to me too. There's no one gone missing I either knew or heard about back then."

"Are there any rumors you heard going around about who it could have been?"

"No. Everybody I've spoken to about it is as clueless as me."

Devlin watched Berry take a sip of red wine and place the glass back down. His study was a man cave. Full of books, papers, cables, and discarded hoodies strewn over the back of the chair and couch.

"Avery is a strange place, Father. And there's that little cabal at the center of it all."

"What cabal?"

"Detective Hennessy, his wife, and O'Neil. The unholy trinity."

"Are you saying they had something to do with it?"

Berry laughed softly. "Yeah, maybe that's a stretch too far. They may not be murderers, but I'll bet they have some secrets between them. And I certainly don't think any of them would be interested in helping an outsider like yourself. Like I say, Avery is a strange place, Father Devlin. Sometimes I think it's like a crooked version of Shangri La. A little town full of secrets cut off from the world."

"Boston's less than an hour away."

"Yeah. Maybe not that cut off."

"I'd better make a move." Devlin rose to leave and Berry swung forward in his chair and stood, glass still in hand.

"One other thing I wanted to ask..." said Devlin.

"Sure."

"You're definite Father O'Neil was out walking in the middle of the night."

"I'd swear to it. It was the exact same time I was up at Holy Cross looking for an opportunity to break in."

"And he went up to Oak Ridge?"

"Yeah. I'd wait in my car at the side of the road and watch him with his flashlight. He'd walk out past the lake and head up to the forest. He'd be away for a couple of hours. I'd see his flashlight up there."

"You're sure?"

"Like I said, I'd swear to it."

"Okay. Thanks."

"No problem. Thanks for the letters. I really appreciate it."

"Just look at it as a second chance. Second chances come around once a lifetime."

"Yeah. I guess they do. And I guess I made a lousy burglar."

"I wouldn't give up the day job."

25

I t was late by the time Devlin got back to Holy Cross. He pulled up outside the rectory and got out of the car. For a minute he stood and surveyed the dark shapes of the landscape that stretched out around the church. While he looked out, he put his hands into his pocket and felt the small, hard round form of the chestnut he'd picked up in the study. He took it out and twiddled it around in his fingers absentmindedly.

Holy Cross was relatively high up, built on the rising ground that climbed up from the town of Avery below to the forests above. The view from the front of the church took in the lights of the town nestled in the bottom of the valley. Main Street and the blocks of shops, offices, and residential housing radiating outward were outlined by streetlights, window lights, and traffic headlights.

But the view from the side of the church, where Devlin was now standing, was different. It was dark and quiet. An expanse of fields and forest that spread out beneath the moon and stars.

Devlin's private contemplation was broken by a flash in his peripheral vision. He turned to see the cone of a flashlight traveling over the gravel pathway and recognized the dark bulky figure holding it; Hoyt Tanner, the sexton.

Tanner approached Devlin and stopped a few feet short of him, switching off his flashlight.

"Evening, Father."

"Hoyt."

"Everything okay?"

"Yeah. I was just looking at the view."

Tanner nodded and turned to look out over the countryside. "It's restful to look at, ain't it?"

"Where were you before you came to Avery?" asked Devlin.

"I was working as a ranger in Selden Neck State Park over in Connecticut."

"Why did you move?"

"I retired. My daughter and son-in-law live nearby. I came to be close to them."

"You got to know the place yet?"

"Got my bearings I think." Tanner's eye was caught by the chestnut Devlin was toying with. "What's that you've got there?"

"This? Oh, an old chestnut is all. Found it in the study."

"Thought so. You mind if I take a look?"

"Really? You wanna look at this?"

"Yeah. I do. That looks like an American chestnut to me."

Devlin handed the chestnut to Tanner who looked it over.

"It is. This is an American chestnut. Where did you say you got it?"

"Father O'Neil picked it up on a walk."

"You know these are rare now?" Tanner chuckled to himself. "'Course, I worked in national parks most of my life, but I guess it's something most people wouldn't know about. Used to be millions of American Chestnut trees but they were all blighted. Hardly any of 'em left. All Japanese chestnut trees now. Looks like Father O'Neil found one of the last American chestnut trees in Massachusetts. Probably why he kept it. What're the words written on it?"

"It's Latin, 'I love you, forgive me.' Don't know anything else about it."

Tanner handed the chestnut back to Devlin.

"Well, I'll wish you good night, Father."

"Goodnight."

Devlin stood awhile longer looking at the chestnut and then out over the fields in darkness and the woods up in Oak Ridge. He thought about the rumors regarding Father O'Neil that Berry had mentioned. About Berry seeing O'Neil out on midnight walks to the forest. It struck Devlin again as utterly strange behavior for a man in his sixties enfeebled with cancer.

Devlin's cell buzzed. It was Sarah.

"Hi."

"Hi, Father, sorry it's late but I had to ring someone. I called the police station for an update and got through to a lieutenant there. He said they'd just spoken to the adoption agency. The agency came back with a name for my brother. Stephen Martin." There was a pause and Sarah cleared her throat. "His name was Stephen Martin. He was born in 1997. As soon as the cops got his details from the agency they checked police records and they got a hit. They found a file on him and there was a note on it from a police officer in Boston who found Stephen sleeping on the streets. The note said he had a small amount of amphetamines on him. The officer confiscated the drugs but didn't arrest him due to the small amount. Instead, he called an outreach officer who tried to get him into a hostel for the night, but Stephen refused. Then he managed to get away, and they lost him. The note was dated January 2012, so he would have been around fifteen. That can't have been long before he died."

"Have the cops found out anything else about him?"

"Nothing yet. But I called you... Well, because I called back and asked Hennessy what they were going to do next and he kind of clammed up. He got all tetchy with me and told me to leave it to him, and that if there were any developments he'd call me. It was kind of abrupt. I just don't know what to do with this... It's overwhelming... What should we do next, Father?"

Devlin's mind ran through different possibilities about what they could do with this new information. Then he glanced down at the chestnut in his hand that had taken Tanner's interest, and the answer hit him like lightning.

"Can I come over? I have something to show you. Something you might know more about than me."

26

"You came to ask me about a chestnut tree?"

"I came to ask the head of the Avery Conservation society about a very rare chestnut tree. The same person who told me she was involved in just about every local group in Avery."

Devlin reached into his pocket, pulled out the chestnut, and threw it to Sarah, who caught it and inspected it.

"What does the writing mean?"

"It's Latin, '*ambo te ignosce me,*' it means 'I love you, forgive me.' It's Father O'Neil's. He picked it up on walks up to Oak Ridge."

"Oak Ridge? That's a hell of a journey for a man in O'Neil's condition. That's gotta be a five mile walk. We did half that walk when we went up around the lake and it wasn't easy going."

"Yeah. And I think I know why he's doing it."

"Why?"

"Like the words on the chestnut say, '*I love you, forgive me.*' He's going all the way out there for some kind of penance. Something up there means something to him. Tanner the sexton told me the chestnut is from an American Chestnut tree, which is very rare."

"They are. They don't survive anymore and there are hardly any left, so about three years ago we planted half a dozen as a project. I went up there to help plant them. It's a kind of secret. The trees are vulnerable to blight and need to be protected."

"Where are they?"

"Up at Oak Ridge forest, on private land."

"Who owns it?"

"Tony Driscoll."

"Does he own everything in this town?"

"He owns a lot. But why are you convinced there's anything up there?"

"Lots of reasons to do with O'Neil and my conviction he's a man haunted by something. But some of it has to do with your dreams. You dreamed you were being buried. You saw the symbol above your brother's grave in the crypt. There was a connection all along between you and your brother. It's as if he was telling you where he lay. And, like I said before, I think your dreams have even more to show us than they already have."

"Like what?"

"You said you kept seeing the tops of trees in a forest and night changing into day and back again."

"You think there's another body up there?"

"Maybe. Just give me directions, doesn't matter if they're rough, I'll find..."

"I'm coming too."

"You really don't have to."

"It's too difficult to give you directions. It's half a dozen trees beyond a fence on the east side of Oak Ridge. It'll be a hell of a job finding them in the dark if you don't know the way. If I go too I'll remember when we get up there. If I don't, you'll be there all damn night. And besides, they're my dreams, not yours."

They took Devlin's car and drove along the turnpike, taking a right across the forest. They traveled the forest road for a couple of miles until Sarah told Devlin to pull over by an old bridge that spanned a tricking stream. When they got out, Devlin found a flashlight in the trunk and handed it to Sarah.

"There's a path along the forest floor that leads to the edge of Driscoll's land," said Sarah. "Follow me."

The moon was high, full, and bright, and the cloudless night revealed a dome of stars. The temperature had dropped and it felt like a frost was on the way.

They skirted the lake, and just as they reached the fringe of the forest Sarah suddenly halted.

"What is it?" asked Devlin.

"I think there's something in the woods."

Devlin squinted as Sarah ran her flashlight back and forth. "I don't see anything."

Sarah shrugged. "Must have been a fox or something. Place will be riddled with them. Let's keep going, it's not far from here."

Sarah led with the flashlight and Devlin followed a few feet behind. They traveled deeper into the woodland where it was even darker and where they were forced to move with more care, looking out for the shrubs, rocks, and exposed roots on the ground. They came to a low wooden fence that marked the boundary of Driscoll's land. They hopped the fence and walked on till Sarah stopped and Devlin came to a halt by her side.

"There." Sarah was pointing the flashlight up to a cluster of trees, all about twenty feet high. Their branches were bare except for the odd dead brown leaf still clinging on.

"Think this is it," said Sarah. Walking in a small circle, she moved her flashlight in a large arc around them. "This is the place O'Neil came to but it doesn't look like there's much here to me."

"He came here up for a reason. I'm sure of it. Maybe it was on the way to someplace else."

"My God... Look... Look at that..." Sarah had pointed her flashlight at the bough of a tree a few feet away from the chestnuts. Painted on the bough were seven yellow lines, like snakes, or a simplified sketch of a tree.

Devlin studied the painted lines up close. Then he walked under the tree, looking up at the mesh of branches belonging to other trees nearby. He stopped, squatted, and surveyed the forest floor.

"Stand still."

The voice was gruff and harsh, and took Devlin and Sarah by surprise. They turned to see Tony Driscoll in a long, thick overcoat, boots, and a peak cap. He had a shotgun raised.

"What the hell are you doing here?" barked Driscoll.

"Sorry," said Sarah. "We were just out walking and didn't see any signs."

Driscoll lowered his shotgun and strode up to Sarah. "You're lying. There are signs all over the place. And it's midnight. You're hunting on my land."

"Hunting? That's ridiculous. We don't have any guns," said Sarah. "It's an honest..."

"I saw you from my jeep on the turnpike, your flashlights giving you away like a pair of prize assholes. You're on private land and you know it."

Driscoll approached Devlin, still holding his shotgun across his body.

"Father Devlin. We meet again. I've been waiting to get some time alone with you. Ever since you insulted my family at my son's wedding. And ever since you got me pulled in by the cops 'cos of what happened to my family's tomb. By God, I ought to whip you for the inconvenience you've caused me."

Devlin eyed the gun and Driscoll's twitching hands. He

sensed the moment of violence was approaching and knew there'd be no avoiding it.

"You should work on your manners," said Devlin.

"You son-of-a-bitch..."

Driscoll's fingers tensed around the shotgun barrel and Devlin didn't hesitate. He went low, fast, shifting his weight onto his left leg, the whoosh of the rifle butt missing his face by millimeters. He grabbed hold of Driscoll's moving arm and snapped out his right leg, driving the edge of his foot into Driscoll's knee. Driscoll's leg collapsed beneath him and his body buckled and dropped to the ground. Devlin wasn't sure if Driscoll's knee was broken but he was definitely incapacitated.

Devlin pulled the shotgun out of Driscoll's grasp and watched him writhe on the floor.

"You asshole..." Driscoll screamed. "I'll hang you up and cut off your balls..."

"Get up..." ordered Devlin. "I said, get up,"

Driscoll got to his feet and hobbled backward from Devlin. Now unarmed he was a good deal less sure of himself.

"I didn't know this was your land," Devlin lied. "Now I do, we'll leave."

"Give me my shotgun."

"You can come get it from me at the church." Devlin swung the shotgun in Driscoll's direction. "Now you head on back to your jeep before something happens you can't walk away from."

"You arrogant piece of crap. I'll call the police and have your asses thrown in jail ." Driscoll was yelling now but he was still retreating. "You're new here and you've made a big mistake. A huge mistake. You don't know who you're dealing with. I'll be back with others, a gang of us, and we'll mess you up so bad..."

Driscoll hurled more threats as he limped backward, occasionally stumbling, until he turned and disappeared into the distant night.

Devlin turned to Sarah. "You okay?"

"Yeah. I think so. That was scary. Where did you learn to fight like that?"

"In all the fights I lost. Can you hand me the flashlight?"

Devlin had crouched down and was studying the ground. She handed him his flashlight and he began sweeping it over the earth, passing it over an area of about twenty foot. Then he stood up and began walking and sweeping the flashlight from side to side. Sarah watched Devlin go back and forth before returning to where she was standing.

"What is it?" asked Sarah.

"There are depressions in the soil. Where the ground has been disturbed and given way slightly. Here..."

Sarah took the flashlight and roamed its white bar over the ground. Devlin was right. Though a light smattering of shrubs obscured it, there were long, narrow depressions of between five and six feet in the clearing between a ring of trees. A wave of awful realization swept over Sarah.

"You think they're... graves? Don't you? Like the body in the old church."

"I'd bet my faith on it."

"We should call the police."

"Yeah. But I'd like to make sure we're calling the cops out for a good reason. There are shovels back at the church for the sexton. I'm going to drive back and get one. I'll drop you off at your apartment."

"No. I'll come with you."

"It's late..."

"I'll come with you. I'm part of all this now. You'll need help."

They drove back to the church, picked up the shovels, and arrived back at the cluster of chestnuts. The depressions in the ground were in a very rough line, so they chose to start digging in the dip with the least shrubbery. In turns, one of them would stand holding a flashlight while the other dug a trench at the head of the dip, shoveling the top soil with energy and attack at first and then, as they got two or three feet down, slowing through a mixture of fatigue and caution due to the dense clay subsoil. Though they feared that Driscoll and his men would return at any time, he didn't come back.

It didn't take too long before something began to appear, glimpses of a pale material peeping out from the dirt. They both crouched, Sarah holding the flashlight and Devlin gently teasing the layers of soil away.

"Dear God," said whispered.

Staring out of the ground were the dark eye-sockets of a skull filled in with soil. Though his fingers were frozen, Devlin carried on scooping and picking away the clay soil, eventually revealing more of the skull and the upper vertebrae that formed the neck.

"What are you doing?" asked Sarah. "We know it's a skull."

"There's something I need to see."

Devlin stopped scraping away the earth and grabbed the flashlight, focusing it on the lower part of the skull.

"What is it?" asked Sarah.

"The hyoid bone is broken. Like the body in the old crypt."

"What does that mean?"

"Maybe that, whoever this is, was strangled like the other victim."

Sarah stood and surveyed the other dips in the ground. She shivered from the bitter night and the thought of the poor souls buried away in this silent place.

"Time to call the police."

BY DAWN, the area was taped off, covered in mist, and crawling with police, forensics, and dogs.

Sarah had left for her bed just after the first officers arrived. Devlin was still at the site of the graves. He was standing a good way back from the tape looking on silently, his tired face drawn and his eyes dark with thought.

"You should go back, Father."

Detective Hennessy was standing in front of him. Devlin hadn't noticed him approaching and that made him realize how tired he must be. He glanced at his watch. It was just after six. He had morning Mass to prepare.

"Yeah, I really should. How many graves are there?"

"Three... We think. At least the dogs haven't located anymore."

"How many have they opened up?"

"Only one fully. It's slow work."

"It's the same as the body in the old crypt?"

"It's too early to say. We've got Driscoll down the station for questioning. You should get some sleep. Leave the investigation to the professionals."

"You still think it's Driscoll? What about the yellow painting on the tree?"

"You leave those questions to the proper authorities. We have a hell of a lot of manpower on this now. Why were you up here, Father? In the middle of the night?"

Devlin paused. He thought about telling Hennessy the whole story. Then he thought about what Berry had said. About the unholy trinity.

"I was out walking," he replied. "I was just out walking."

DEVLIN WALKED BACK through the woods and stopped at the top of the slope down to the lake. From where he was standing he could see the town of Avery nestled in the valley, the town's lights still on. He lit up a cigar, inhaled the smoke deep down into his grateful lungs, and reflected.

Now there were four bodies, and apparently no one in Avery had ever noticed even one person go missing. He took another toke and watched the town waking up, this quiet little town that at that moment, it seemed to Devlin, to be quietly ashamed of itself.

Devlin trudged back across the fields finishing his cigar, his head fuzzy and his eyes sore. When he got to Holy Cross it still wasn't fully light. The church looked completely at peace without a soul about. He dug into his coat pocket, pulled out his keys, and realized the door was already open.

Carefully, Devlin pushed at the door and stepped into the hall. None of the lights inside were on. He walked along the hall and checked the living room and kitchen, which were both empty. Then he checked the study.

Sitting in the armchair by the window, in the cold blue half-light of the morning, was an emaciated, jaundiced figure with pain etched into his face and seething indignation in his small eyes.

"You wretched man."

It was Father O'Neil.

27

"I had my grave misgivings about you, Father Devlin, from the start. But even I didn't believe you would stoop so slow."

Devlin was sitting in a wooden chair placed against the wall opposite O'Neil. It seemed to Devlin that the older man was now transforming. Cancer and the surgery had a good deal to do with it. But even that didn't explain how ravaged and aged he had become, his body wizened and fragile, like the branch of a tree that was dying, knotted, and shrunken. Like a man being eaten from the inside out by something ravenous and unstoppable.

"You stole from me. You stole personal and sensitive correspondence from a sick, incapable man."

"I destroyed them. Like you were supposed to do."

"I didn't ask you to do that for me," barked O'Neil at the top of his thin voice, his eyes bulging with anger.

"So report me."

"You know damn well I can't report you, because those letters are supposed to be confidential and entrusted to me. You, Father Devlin, have no sense of personal duty or obligation and involve yourself in affairs that are best left to people with more judgment and who actually possess ethical standards. The sooner I return from this hellish recovery and take the church back from you, the better for everyone. I've already spoken to Bishop Molina, who suggested I could return as soon as next Monday."

The idea that O'Neil, a man finishing a course of chemotherapy, was even remotely ready to pick up his duties was absurd. Devlin let it go. Instead, he leaned forward and stared into O'Neil's eyes.

"I went up to Oak Ridge. To the place you walked to late at night. I found three graves. The police are up there now. Three more graves. Three more murders. You were visiting the graves, weren't you? Who did you love, Francis? Who is it that must forgive you?"

O'Neil genuflected and whispered a 'Merciful Christ.'

"I know you have something to do with the bodies, with the body in the crypt and the ones in the wood. I think you're terrified, Father. Terrified that something from the past has woken and is coming for you."

For a moment O'Neil did look terrified. As if he were looking at his own death. Then he snapped out of it and wrinkled his face into a snarl.

"The only man with a past to be ashamed of in this room is you, Father Devlin."

"What does the yellow symbol mean? The seven snaking lines?"

"I have no idea what you're talking about."

O'Neil reached for his cell, made a call, and impatiently muttered instructions to the person at the other end. He put his cell back in his pocket and eyeballed Devlin.

"My driver is coming to get me. The Bishop, out of the goodness of his heart, has loaned me his chauffeur while I'm getting better." O'Neil stabbed out a finger at Devlin. "It is no coincidence that since you arrived all sorts of wickedness has come to the surface. It's as if you attract evil."

"You're right." Devlin's answer seemed to catch O'Neil by surprise. "I do attract evil. It seems to rise up wherever I go. But it's not evil I created. It's hidden in the long grass, lying in wait, a legacy of the acts of other men. And I will find who these other men are, Father O'Neil. The men from whose acts this evil began to spread. I will bring them to whatever kind of justice they deserve. That's a promise."

O'Neil's driver had appeared and was standing at the door.

"Come in." O'Neil beckoned the man forward who, without needing instruction, helped the aged priest from his chair and supported him out of the study.

Devlin was alone, and for a while he didn't move and stared out the study window. He watched the cemetery in the low, sharp sunlight and listened to the sound of the car taking O'Neil away.

In the silence Devlin felt it again, the certainty of something coming toward him out of the morning mist. A dark and formless shape that took on form and shape as it grew closer. He was certain at that moment that all he needed to do was sit still and the darkness would find him. And he was also certain of what he knew he had to do, just as he had done in Halton Springs, and just as he had done in Sag Harbor. He would reach out, grasp the darkness and, not for one moment, submit to it.

The church bell struck eight and Devlin dragged his tired bones up from the chair to prepare for Mass.

28

A very PD was a wide, one-story red-brick building. Devlin parked in the lot to the side of the precinct and entered the lobby. About half a dozen people were waiting in brown molded-plastic chairs that were fixed to the wall. Devlin approached the records window and asked to speak to Hennessy. When he told the desk Sergeant his name, the officer's eye widened a little in recognition and he called through on the phone. After a few moments the door buzzed open, and a uniformed officer appeared and told Devlin to follow him.

Beyond the lobby, the building turned into a maze of corridors and offices without any overarching design. It was an accumulation of hastily improvised alterations made to meet constantly changing needs.

Devlin was led to a long narrow office that smelled of sweat and burnt filter coffee. Running along the middle of the room was a row of desks placed side-by-side. Dry-erase boards covered with words scrawled in different colors of marker-pen hung along the walls. Detective Ted Hennessy was sitting on the end desk, and Sarah was sitting opposite him.

Hennessy nodded at the officer who left them to it.

"Well, here he is. The man who keeps finding dead people. Take a seat, Father. Miss Wilson was very anxious to have you with her."

"Thanks for coming, Father," said Sarah. "I really appreciate you being here."

"Is there any more information on the bodies?" asked Devlin.

"We got a few more details but the full report won't be for a couple of weeks. Basically, all three bodies are likely male, in their teenage years. All have broken hyoids with no signs of healing. So, broken perimortem."

"That can't be a coincidence," said Devlin.

"No. It can't be," replied Hennessy.

"You have four young men murdered over a period of maybe ten or fifteen years using the same M.O. That's a serial killer."

"And that's why the FBI have flown in to assist the Bureau and local law enforcement. We're looking at a murderer who targets and picks up boys on the street. Maybe he's been following them. Maybe for weeks and even months. These boys, they're the perfect victims. Alone, vulnerable, and unlikely to be reported missing."

"But why are they ending up buried in a forest in Avery?"

"For the same reason we had a bootlegging trail through here. Same reason Driscoll runs his haulage and possibly other shadier business out of here. We're small, out of the way, and right by the freeway to Boston."

"You can't still think it's Driscoll?" said Devlin.

"Damn right I do."

"Is that what the Bureau thinks?"

"Yeah, it is. And if it isn't Driscoll then it's someone who worked for Driscoll. He had the drugs operation going out of the old church. The bodies were on his land. He looks pretty good for this. But I shouldn't say anymore." Hennessy paused for a moment and seemed to be weighing up whether to reveal anything further. "What I will tell you is that these bodies are more recent than your brother's, Miss Wilson. The most recent is about a year old and from scraps of material we found it seems like he was wrapped in a linen shawl and then buried. And there is one advantage we have now."

"What?" asked Sarah.

"The FBI. They fast-tracked a DNA test and we got a hit."

"Who?"

Hennessy turned his screen toward Devlin and Sarah. On the screen was the image of a young, dark-haired boy of about fourteen. It was a photo on a charge sheet for assault.

"Luke Weber. When he was processed he was swabbed."

"Is he from round here?" asked Devlin.

"Nope. It says he had no address, permanent or temporary; he was homeless. I haven't found anything about where he's from or next of kin yet. This charge sheet from a year ago is all we currently have. It was issued by a cop up in Portland."

"And somehow he ended up dead in Avery," said Devlin.

"That's what it looks like."

"Both boys, Stephen and Luke, had some sort of police record putting them away from Avery?"

"Yeah."

"That's interesting, isn't it? A fortunate coincidence."

"I don't think so. The kids were young and living on the streets, and just the kind of individuals that come into contact with law enforcement or other agencies. Anyway, this investigation is pretty much out of my hands now. It's between the guys down from Worcester Homicide Bureau and the FBI. They run the show. I'm just a mere cog in a much mightier machine. Now, I need to get on with very boring non-homicide-related paperwork. I should show you out."

On the steps of the precinct, Devlin and Sarah absorbed the new information.

"What the hell is going on?" asked Sarah. "Four bodies now? All of them young boys? All of them died the same way? But none of them are from round here?"

"And now the Feds and Homicide are all over it we won't get any more intel from Hennessy. I have to confront Father O'Neil again. He's part of all of this but I can't crack him open."

"Why don't you say that to Hennessy?"

"I don't trust Detective Ted Hennessy."

"Why not?"

"Because I don't believe he's dealing a straight hand. And though he says it's all out of his hands, he'll still be the source for local, on-the-ground intelligence for the entire investigation."

29

Bishop Molina had a chauffeured car at his disposal for office hours and to take him to and from work-related functions. It was part of a life built around his comfort; a palatial residence in Worcester, regular business class trips to Rome, and a budget available to him of nearly forty million dollars. A less entitled man might feel shame at such an embarrassment of riches.

Molina took up nearly half of the rear seat. Sitting inches away from him, gazing thoughtfully out of the window, was Father Deeney.

"You're sure," Deeney began thoughtfully, "that O'Neil is really up to going back to Holy Cross? I mean, he is very, very frail."

"He's recovering. Obviously, it will take time but he's going in the right direction."

"The man's at death's door."

"He's on the mend and as determined as I am that he get back to Holy Cross. I've rounded up a group of volunteers to help him with the duties," Molina added, almost in a whisper.

"He won't actually have to do anything. And then we'll be rid of Devlin."

"What is it you dislike so much about Father Devlin?"

"He's an arrogant trouble-maker, a bad priest, and I didn't choose him. He's out to cause as many problems as he can. Controversy follows him wherever he goes. I could go on."

"He wasn't responsible for the body in the old crypt. Or the bodies in the woods."

"Wasn't he?"

"You think he's a murderer?" said Deeney in astonishment. "You can't be serious?"

"No, I don't think he's a murderer. But there's something about that man, something disturbed, like a disease, that draws unhappiness and disorder toward him."

"I agree there's a very forceful spirit about him. I find him quite fascinating."

"I spoke to Father O'Neil before we left. Apparently he saw Devlin this morning. He said Devlin upset him terribly."

"What did he say?"

"He wouldn't tell me. But he was in a terrible state."

The car had drawn up outside O'Neil's house. Deeney got out and stood on the drive for a minute waiting for the Bishop to hoist himself out and join him. As they reached the door, another car turned onto the drive and stopped. O'Neil's sister, Patricia, a thin woman with her gray hair in a bun and wearing a jacket and tweed skirt, got out and hurried toward them. She pulled out her keys from her handbag and smiled apologetically.

"I'll let you in, Bishop Molina. He's expecting you."

"Thank you, Patricia."

Patricia returned to the car to unpack groceries from the boot while the Bishop and Deeney stepped into the house.

"Father O'Neil?" Deeney called out. "It's Bishop Molina and Father Deeney."

There was no reply. The two men entered the empty living room and looked at each other. Deeney pointed a finger upwards and whispered 'in bed' to Molina. Molina nodded and Patricia entered, her hands full with grocery bags.

"He's still in bed?" she said.

"It looks that way," Deeney replied. "Why don't I go and see if I can gently rouse him? You have your hands full."

Patricia nodded. "Thank you, Father."

While Deeney went upstairs Molina sank into an armchair and watched Patricia buzz back and forth, carrying in the shopping through the lounge to put away in the kitchen.

A few minutes passed and eventually Deeney returned alone. He stood in the doorway to the lounge looking grave and pale.

"Is he coming?" asked Molina impatiently.

"I think you need to come with me."

"What is it?"

"You need to come with me now. It's Father O'Neil. Something terrible has happened."

Molina, picking up on Deeney's urgency, got to his feet with surprising speed and followed him.

Halfway up the stairs Deeney turned to the Bishop and said quietly, "Prepare yourself. It's quite distressing."

"I'm a Bishop. I've seen dead people before."

Deeney didn't answer. He led the way to the landing and pointed to the loft hatch above them. The square hatch was open and an old wooden ladder was propped against it. Molina stepped forward and looked up. Just visible and framed by the wooden hatch were two legs swinging gently. Wind whistled through the gaps in the roof and the beams creaked.

"Dear Christ," said Molina quietly.

Suddenly a scream ripped through the house. They turned to see Patricia O'Neil collapsed on the stairs, sobbing and heaving with shock.

30

The first car to arrive was Detective Hennessy's.

Bishop Molina was standing at the window watching the detective park and get out. He saw another car, a red Honda sedan, pull up behind Hennessy's. Devlin and a young woman climbed out. They and the detective had a short conversation, then Hennessy carried on up the drive while Devlin and the young woman waited.

"I don't believe it," said Molina.

Deeney was sitting on the couch attempting to console an inconsolable Patricia O'Neil. "What? What is it?"

"It's Hennessy. He's here with Devlin."

The doorbell rang and Deeney went to let Hennessy in. Over Patricia O'Neil's low moans Molina heard them make introductions and Hennessy offer his condolences. Deeney then returned to the living room with Hennessy in tow.

"I think you know Father O'Neil's sister, Patricia," said Deeney.

"I do, very well. Patricia, I'm heartbroken and so sorry for your loss."

For the first time since her brother's death, Patricia spoke. "Thank you, Ted."

Hennessy stepped forward and rubbed her shoulder tenderly.

"This is Bishop Molina," said Deeney.

"Detective, what the hell is Father Devlin doing here?" said Molina, fit to burst with anger.

"Apparently he was coming over to see Father O'Neil."

"Does he know?"

"I informed him about Father O'Neil's passing. But of course, gave no details." Hennessy stood awkwardly for a moment. "I should take a look at the body."

"Upstairs. In the loft," said Deeney.

Molina stood by the window listening to the sobs of Patricia O'Neil, Deeney's consolations, and the footsteps of the detective climbing the stairs. He peered out at Devlin, standing in front of the house with the young woman, and felt his anger boil over. There was something about Devlin, something that clawed at his guts, an instinctive, irrational repulsion and fear that Molina felt in his blood and marrow. And he suspected Devlin knew it. That was the worst thing. That arrogant fool knew how he made Molina feel. He could no longer stand the intense claustrophobia of the house and the O'Neil woman's hysteria. Without a word, Molina left the living room and made for the front door.

The cold air woke him up from a numb stupor and he strode toward Devlin.

"You might as well know that Father O'Neil hanged himself today."

Devlin and the woman looked at each other in horror.

"Myself and Father Deeney found him."

"He hanged himself?" said Devlin, as if he were unable to believe it.

"That's what I said, isn't it? His sister is in pieces. Utterly distraught. He said he spoke to you this morning and was extremely upset. What on earth did you say to him?"

"Wait," said Sarah. "You're not blaming Father Devlin?"

"What did you say to him?" Molina repeated.

"He said he was determined to return to Holy Cross next Monday. But you knew that."

"Yes. And if you think you're staying on at Holy Cross you're profoundly mistaken. Since you came here you've unearthed corpses that had been lain to rest..."

"Murdered. They were murdered... Including my brother..." Sarah protested.

"I hold you, Father Devlin, responsible for Father O'Neil's death. For taking some kind of twisted delight in bringing past pain to good people. I will do everything I can to get you out of this town."

"If you want to get me out of Holy Cross you'll have to go above Cardinal Hermes' head."

"I'll do whatever I have to. I have friends in the highest places."

The three fell silent and watched as a police cruiser and an ambulance pulled up. Hennessy, hearing the sirens, came scurrying out of the house to talk to the officers and paramedics who were disembarking onto the pavement. Then the officers and medics entered the house and Hennessy approached Devlin, Bishop Molina, and Sarah.

"We should find Patricia somewhere to stay, where she can be looked after," said Hennessy.

"She'll stay at my residence where she can be properly comforted and cared for," said Molina.

Hennessy looked at Devlin, then at Molina, and nodded. "Fine. I'll leave it with you to make those arrangements."

"The Bishop says Father O'Neil hanged himself," said Devlin.

"Did he? I see..." Hennessy looked faintly annoyed by Molina's indiscretion. "Yes. That's right."

"Do you have any idea about a time of death?" asked Devlin.

"A couple of hours at a guess. Poor guy, he must have been in a terrible place to take his own life."

"He didn't take his own life," said Devlin.

"What?" replied an astonished Hennessy.

"I said, he didn't take his own life."

"What on earth are you talking about?" Molina bellowed, his whole frame shaking.

"You know as well as I do that he wouldn't take his own life. Father O'Neil was one of the most traditional priests I've ever met. I doubt he agreed with one word of the Catechism and would still regard suicide as a sin."

"You know nothing about that man's beliefs, his faith..." said Molina.

"And he'd just come through grueling surgery and treatment. When he spoke to me this morning he was determined to get back to work next week. Getting back to his church, and getting me out, was the one thing keeping him alive."

"You think he was killed?" asked Hennessy in disbelief.

"I'm saying he didn't take his own life."

Molina exploded with rage, rounding on Devlin and stabbing a finger at his face. "Shut up! For God's sake, shut up! Only feet away from us a man is dead, hanging from a rope. Just keep your undisciplined, unfeeling thoughts to yourself so we all can grieve."

Molina swung away from Devlin and marched back to the house.

"He's right," said Hennessy. "It's insensitive in the circumstances."

Devlin said nothing. He seemed so caught up in his thoughts he didn't appear to even hear Hennessy.

"Did you find anymore out about the bodies up in the woods, detective?" asked Sarah.

"We got two more DNA and ID hits. So far none of them are from Avery. Like your brother Stephen and the other kid, Luke Weber, who had a rap sheet in Portland, they all have records with social services or police files that put them in other parts of the state."

"So all four kids have records putting them somewhere solid and away from Avery?" asked Devlin, who had snapped out of whatever thoughts had been consuming him.

"Yeah. All the kids are homeless, on the streets, and in some kind of trouble. The records span about ten years so far. Stephen was the earliest record and Luke Weber was the most recent. Nearest one was a kid, Joshua McCleary, who was down in Providence about three years ago."

"What was the record on him?"

"Social services. A priest had rung it in from a church in Greenfield."

"Which church?"

Hennessy shrugged. "I don't remember. Blessed something, or maybe not, I can't recall off-hand... It's a goddamned mystery how they all ended up here, never mind how they died."

"Do any of the boys found at Oak Ridge have next-of-kin?" asked Sarah.

"We've tracked down one family member. But the victims were either orphans or came from broken homes and hadn't been in touch with their family for years." Hennessy looked around anxiously at a forensics crime scene vehicle that had pulled up. "I gotta go talk to the medics and let them know forensics are here."

Hennessy returned to the house. Devlin and Sarah got back into her car.

Sarah pulled out and began driving back toward Avery. "Hennessy was right. What you said was a little insensitive."

"I was insensitive? Molina did pretty much blame me for the murder of the boys."

"Fair point."

"I'm telling you now, Father O'Neil didn't take his own life."

"So, what? Someone murdered him?"

"Yeah."

"Why?"

"Because he couldn't be trusted with whatever he knew about the murdered boys. With whatever it was he wouldn't tell me."

31

It was late to be making a cross-state trip. Yet, ever since Devlin had spoken to Hennessy earlier in the day he'd had a feeling. A feeling that had grown into something that was burning away inside him. Something that couldn't be put off.

Once he'd gotten onto Route 2 it wasn't so bad. The highway took him in a straight line east to west across the state and then onto the 2A into Greenfield. Hennessy had told Devlin the church was 'The Blessed something' in Greenfield, and that had been enough to locate The Blessed Sacrament. He'd rung ahead but couldn't get hold of the priest and had spoken to a deacon instead. He told the deacon it was about the murdered boy that the Greenfield priest had reported. He asked that the priest return his call at the first opportunity. But the priest didn't get back. Devlin could have left it and tried again the next day, but now he had a burning intent, like a holy fire, so it couldn't wait. He had to get in his car and look this priest right in the eye.

Devlin drove into downtown Greenfield, took a right on Main Street, and pulled up outside The Blessed Sacrament. The church stood opposite the courthouse on a small island of green. It was a narrow red brick building, early twentieth century, with Gothic influences and narrow, dark windows.

Inside, the church was empty. Devlin dabbed the holy water, genuflected, and walked down the aisle. He knelt and took a seat on the front bench, then waited and prayed for a while. No one appeared so he ventured around the back of the church and found a small cottage out back with some lights on. He knocked, and after a few moments the priest appeared. Devlin instantly realized that he had met him before and that when he'd looked up the name of the priest at The Blessed Sacrament, he hadn't put it together.

"Father Lopez?" said Devlin.

"Yes?"

"We met before. I'm Father Devlin from Holy Cross in Avery. You came to my church last week with Bishop Molina and Father Deeney. We met in the church hall."

"Oh, yes. I remember. I asked to shadow the Bishop for a day."

Lopez was a young priest, still in his twenties, with slicked-down black hair and a mustache he'd possibly cultivated, guessed Devlin, for the much older congregation he served. He was tall and looked in good shape, athletic, though he seemed unsettled by Devlin's appearance.

"The deacon told me you called. It's about the boys they found in Avery, isn't it? I haven't had time to return your call, it's been such a busy day. What's happened in Avery, it's just awful."

"Yes, it is."

"What can I do for you?"

"I just need a few minutes to discuss the matter of the boy you reported, Joshua McCleary."

Lopez sighed and looked at his watch. "Father Devlin, it's

really very late and... Well, I have an early Mass, as I'm sure you do too. I don't have anything to tell you that I haven't already told the police."

Devlin shrugged. "Okay. Sure. I understand. Say, is there any chance I could take five minutes to warm up and use the bathroom? It's an hour-and-a-half drive from Avery and I'm beat."

Reluctantly Lopez agreed and as Devlin breached the threshold he casually threw out a request for a cup of coffee, just to keep him alert on the drive back. Lopez, though frustrated by Devlin's creeping imposition, agreed.

On the way back from the bathroom to the kitchen, where Lopez was busy making the coffee, Devlin took a moment to peer into the rooms on either side of the hallway. One of the rooms was a study lined with bookcases loaded with theological works. In the middle of the room was a leather recliner, and by the recliner was a side-table with a stack of books piled on it. The object that got Devlin's attention, however, was the copper chain slung over the back of the armchair. Devlin recognized it immediately. It was a cilice, a device worn around the thigh to deliberately cause discomfort, similar to the practice of wearing a hair shirt.

In the kitchen they stood in awkward silence, Devlin holding his warm mug and Lopez empty-handed and agitated.

Devlin raised his mug. "Thank you."

Lopez gave a curt nod.

Devlin looked down into his coffee. "You're right about what you said."

"About what?"

"It's a terrible business in Avery. With all those poor boys being discovered."

"Yes."

"Poor souls. You know, it's odd... so far we have no record of

any of the boys being within forty miles of Avery. Any of them.
Yet here they are, murdered and buried in the ground in a town
they apparently never visited. Don't you think that's strange?"

"I'm sure the police will be aware of this and are doing all
they can to find out why those boys ended up where they
did."

Devlin frowned for a moment and looked at Lopez.

"Something wrong, Father?" asked Lopez.

"No, no." He took a gulp of coffee. "Thanks for this."

"You're welcome.

"The boy you called the social services about, Joshua..."

"I told the police everything I know..."

"I know you did. But just so I'm clear. He was sleeping in the
church grounds?"

"Yes."

"And you didn't know him? Or where he was from? Or where
his family lived?"

"No."

"And social services took it up. Is that right?"

"Yes."

"Did they come down to the church?"

"Excuse me?"

"To find Joshua?"

"I don't know. Possibly. All I know is that I made the call and
then the boy stopped coming to sleep on the grounds of the
church."

"So, the social services may never have seen him?"

"No. But I did. I saw him."

There was a silence. Lopez had crossed his arms tight and
clenched his jaw.

"What did Joshua look like?" asked Devlin.

"Medium height, blonde hair. Dirty. That's all. It was three
years ago."

Devlin nodded, swigged down his coffee, and placed his mug on the countertop.

"Thanks for the pitstop."

Lopez didn't answer. He picked up Devlin's mug and placed it in the sink.

On the way out they passed through the hall where, to Lopez's visible anger, Devlin stopped, loitering to look at the photographs and certificates hanging on the wall.

Devlin pointed to framed certificates that had been hung in a row. "You kick-box?"

"Mixed Martial Arts."

"You compete?"

"No. Obviously not. It's not compatible with my vocation."

"But you train?"

"I'm going to have to be blunt, Father. You pretty much invited yourself into my house and now you have overstayed the small welcome you had."

"You're going to throw me out?"

Lopez's mouth twitched and he fisted his hands. "No. Don't be absurd. I'm anxious to get to bed."

"Sure. I understand. Oh, wow..."Devlin pointed to a certificate that hung pride of place in the middle of the collection of framed pictures. "You have a Doctors in Divinity?"

"Yes."

"Impressive. How long have you been at The Blessed Sacrament?"

"Five years. I run three churches across west Massachusetts."

Devlin continued scanning the wall and saw a photograph that made him smile. It was of Lopez and a much larger, older man. They were shaking hands.

"Bishop Molina," said Devlin.

"He came to my graduation at Boston University."

Devlin smiled. "I'm sorry for the intrusion. I'm going."

Devlin stepped out into the front yard and pulled out a cigar, lighting it up.

"Terrible habit, I know."

"Goodnight, Father." Lopez pushed the door shut but Devlin put his foot on the threshold, stopping the door from closing.

"What the hell are you doing...?" said Lopez.

"'They'll be doing all they can to find out why those boys ended up where they did.'"

"What?"

"That's what you said, Father. 'They'll be doing all they can to find out why those boys ended up where they did.'"

"So what?"

Devlin took a suck on his cigar. "It almost makes it sound like it was their fault, the boys."

"That's not what I meant. Now get your foot out of my door before I call the police."

Devlin started up the car and headed back down Main Street, smoking his cigar down as he drove. Just as he began to turn left he saw headlights moving in his rearview mirror. A car had moved out from the side of the road not far from where he had been parked.

At the next set of lights, he slowed a little to catch the stop signal and looked in his rearview again. The same car, a black Mercedes, stopped two cars behind. The lights went green and Devlin carried onto Route 2 with the Mercedes tailing him all the way back from Greenfield to Avery.

Devlin pulled up outside Holy Cross and waited, watching the Mercedes slow then turn off the main road and disappear into the night. Who, wondered Devlin, had taken an interest in his trip out to Greenfield? Was it one of the people he'd provoked or angered since he'd arrived in Avery?

But Devlin was tired and not much interested in more guess-work. Besides, he'd already decided on his next move. After

Father O'Neil's death, there was only one other door to knock on. And he had to move as fast as he could, as fast as his duties at Holy Cross permitted, at least. Now there were four bodies, one only a year old, and there was no reason why, in time, the killer wouldn't strike again.

32

He'd been picked up for shoplifting. It was hardly anything. Just a bag of Doritos and a carton of ginger snaps. He'd had enough money to buy the items, but the store looked like such an easy target it was impossible to resist. Those looks turned out to be deceiving.

Jamie hadn't bargained on the old lady behind the cash register being such a mean piece of work and with eyes like a hawk. She called the cops right then and there, and when he wouldn't tell the cops who he was or where he lived, they threw him in the back of the cop car.

So far so regular. They tried to book him in and he made it as difficult as he could. He felt sorry for the cop who was processing him. He was an old guy who was trying to be kind. Maybe, thought Jamie, he had kids of his own. Maybe he was thinking how sorry he was for Jamie, how he hoped that if one of his kids was picked up in a similar situation they'd be treated kindly.

Nevertheless, Jamie sure made it difficult for the old guy. He didn't say a word and refused to do anything he was asked until he'd been asked a dozen times in a dozen different ways. The old cop didn't lose his temper once. He sure was patient for a cop. But when he searched Jamie and found his ID, things took a turn for the worse.

Jamie was put in a small waiting area away from where the adults were being booked in. From here he could still see the old cop at his desk who was probably checking the system for Jamie's records. The cop's desk phone rang and he picked up. There was a short conversation and the old cop put the phone down, scratched his head, and turned to look at Jamie. He got up and walked over with a puzzled look, as if he were trying to solve world hunger.

"You know anyone in the force, son?"

"No."

The cop nodded. "Well, someone sure seems to know you." Then he walked back to his desk.

About thirty minutes passed while the boy waited to see what happened next. Finally, the cop was joined by what the boy assumed was another cop, although this one was in a regular suit and tie, and much younger. Though, from the way the old cop acted, it seemed like the young one was way more senior.

The young cop in the suit and tie walked over to the boy.

"It's okay. You can go."

"Go where?"

"Wherever you want. I can take you to Copacabana if you want."

"Who are you?"

"Captain Olusoga. I deal in juvenile cases. I've told the officer that you're okay to go. After all, it was only a tube of Pringles."

"Doritos... and ginger snaps."

"Exactly. Well, you wanna stay here all night and watch the drunks fall in?"

The boy stood and followed the Captain out of the station onto the sidewalk.

"This is my car. I can drive you wherever you need."

"That's okay. I can walk."

The Captain edged a little closer to the boy and pulled out a twenty.

"You need some money? Go on, take it. If you were stealing potato chips and cookies then you need this."

"Nah. It's okay."

"Suit yourself." The Captain put the bill in his pocket and in one quick, smooth move grabbed Jamie's arm, twisting so hard he thought it might break, and pushed him up against the side of the car.

"I know who you are and where you're supposed to be," he hissed into the side of Jamie's face.

"Please, I don't want to go back... They're bad people..."

"You're dead wrong, son. They're good people. Disciplined people who do things the old way, which is the right way. They're the best people for kids like you, a runaway, a liar, and a thief. You took the rings, Jamie, and I guess you sold them too, huh? They were valuable, precious belongings worth thousands of dollars and given only to special ex-students. I'll bet you sold them just as soon as you could. Now stop your whining and get in the car."

With little trouble, the Captain pushed the boy into the back seat and punched him hard in the face. Then he got into the driver's seat, locked the door, and pulled away.

"You're one of them, aren't you?" said the boy, clutching the side of his face. "One of his."

"Damn right. And proud of it. And so should you be."

33

It was late afternoon before Devlin had a chance to leave Holy Cross. He pulled up outside a house on the outskirts of Avery. It was smart and well-kept. The timber exterior was painted in a shade of cream, and the shutters and door were a light gray. There were small well-tended bushes dotted in front of the house and a good couple of acres of neat lawn. The lights were on. Two other cars were parked in the drive.

Devlin rang the bell. After a short delay, footsteps approached and the door opened.

"Father Devlin?" Susan Hennessy stood in the doorway looking surprised and anxious "What is it? Is everything alright?"

"Actually Susan, I don't know that it is. May I come in?"

"I... Well... Of course..."

Devlin followed Susan into the lounge, where he found Ted Hennessy in a lazy boy, bottle in hand and watching the Patriots play the Dolphins. He must have overheard Devlin's name because he managed to look less surprised by Devlin's arrival than his wife had.

"Father. Take a seat. You want a drink? A beer?"

"Father Devlin doesn't drink, Ted," said Susan.

"Oh," said Ted, getting the message loud and clear.

"Coffee then?"

"No. I'm Okay," said Devlin, taking an armchair by the window.

"What can I do for you?" asked Ted amiably. Susan was still hovering in the entrance to the hall, not committing herself to joining the conversation or leaving.

"I wanted to ask about Father O'Neil. You both knew him better than anyone."

Ted and Susan shot each other looks.

"I guess so," said Ted. "He was a very private man, so we only knew him as much as he allowed. If you get my drift."

"I do. So, what I'm going to ask you now isn't easy."

Hennessy took a swig of beer. "How so?"

"I've heard rumors about Father O'Neil. About inappropriate behavior with members of the congregation."

"From who?"

"You know I won't tell you who, Ted."

"From gutless wonders who won't say it to a man's face, that's who. What kind of questions are these anyway? Francis O'Neil is not even in the ground and you come round here —"

"Yes. Yes, I do come round here, Ted. Because the body of a young man was found in my church. Because people have spoken to me about Father O'Neil's behavior. These are serious matters I cannot ignore, so if there's nothing to it then just say there's nothing to it and I'll go and never mention it again. But if there is something to it, then by God you better speak up now and speak up good."

Hennessy's grip on his beer bottle tightened, his knuckles whitening. He was upright in his lazy-boy now and his face flushed red with rage. But he didn't speak.

Instead, Susan Hennessy spoke with barely restrained contempt.

"He never did anything. He never touched anyone. He wouldn't and couldn't have done anything like that. What he did was say stupid things to a young man. Not inappropriate things, just silly, foolish things. There was a seventeen-year-old boy that was part of the congregation. Francis... Father O'Neil used to get... crushes, I guess you'd call them. Infatuations. But it was all completely innocent. Words. Just silly words. He would 'fall in love' is how he'd put it. A family made a complaint. They came to me and we reached a compromise with the family and Bishop Molina. Father O'Neil would spend six months at a treatment center, which he did, and get the help he needed. The family was satisfied with this solution and didn't take it any further. End of story."

"Was that the end of the story?" asked Devlin.

"What do you mean?"

"What about the boy in the old crypt?"

"Are you kidding me?" Ted yelled. "Are you saying you think O'Neil killed the boy? And the ones up in the forest? Jesus Christ, he couldn't lift a goddamned cat."

"Ted..." Susan said, reprimanding her husband for his language.

"Sorry Susan..."

"I'm saying he might have known something about it," said Devlin. "Adam Berry saw him walk out at night up to the forest. Out to the areas where I found the other graves. That's how I found the graves, Ted. I followed where Father O'Neil went."

"Then why didn't you tell me that yesterday morning?"

"Because honestly, I don't know if I can trust you, Ted."

"You evil, evil, wicked man..." Susan Hennessy's thin figure was trembling with fury. Fury directed completely at Devlin. "How dare you, a man who is more a vagrant than a priest, who has no proper faith or Godly respect at all, insult my husband and drag Father O'Neil, whose body is not yet cold, through the mud. That man had more integrity and faith in his little finger than you have in your whole body. I blame you, Father Devlin, for his death. You are the murderer."

Devlin stood and buttoned his coat.

"Is that it? Are you done? Good," said Susan, spitting out each word. "Get out of our house and never come back."

Devlin was being shut down and all paths had been exhausted. So, he took a parting gamble. He'd sworn to Cardinal Hermes he would keep the suspicions about the Holy Cross accounts confidential. But there were more important things at stake. If he used that information now it might help shift the barricade of lies he suspected he was up against.

"I know about the accounts, Susan."

"What?"

"I know money has been skimmed off the top of the church accounts for years. And so do you. I'm truly sorry to come into your house and upset you both. But there are questions I must ask. When you are ready to tell me where that money has gone, I'll be happy to listen. Maybe even forgive whoever it is. I'm leaving, but I'm not going anywhere."

"Get out."

Devlin left the Hennessy's house, got into his car, and was about to start the engine when he saw Ted Hennessy rush out. Hennessy stopped, and stood on the drive staring at Devlin. Devlin got out of his car and the two men faced each other.

"Let's go for a drive," said Hennessy.

Devlin set off in silence heading out of Avery onto the freeway. Hennessy was agitated and overheated. Maybe it was nerves or too many beers, maybe it was too warm in the car for him, but for whatever reason he was sweating. It was the first time Devlin had seen Hennessy without his flight jacket on. He wore a short-sleeved check shirt. It looked pressed and clean on, but still carried a few old food stains on the front and a couple of wine spots on the pocket.

"You said you might be able to forgive?" said Hennessy. "About the church money?"

Devlin nodded. "I did."

"If I tell you... I tell you everything. Maybe we keep this between me and you?"

"I can't make that promise. You know that, Ted. It depends on what you tell me."

Ted didn't answer. They drove on for a stretch.

"But depending on what you tell me," said Devlin, "I'd do everything I could to help whoever took that money. That's as much as I can promise."

"If I told you the truth, maybe you could even just give us a little time. Before... Before any consequences. It wouldn't have to be much. A few weeks, say. So me and Susan could get a head start putting our affairs in order."

Devlin took a turn onto a narrow road as raindrops started to come down in gentle waves. Ted began speaking in a low monotone.

"I didn't know about the funds till a few months ago. Father O'Neil came to me and told me that Susan had been skimming off the church fund for at least five years. That she'd been helping herself to money from the various funds and that, over time, that money had amounted to a hell of a lot."

"How much?"

"Forty... Fifty thousand."

"What did she use the money for?"

"Her mother's medical bills. Her mom's got Motor Neurone disease and needs round-the-clock care. I thought it was being paid for through her insurance and savings. Truth be told, I didn't ask as long as I didn't have to pay." Hennessy turned to

Devlin. "Father, the shameful truth is I didn't do my job as a police officer because I love Susan. She's my world. We don't have kids, that never happened for us, it wasn't in the Lord's plans, so we just have each other. I couldn't let her go to prison, it would have destroyed me and her.

"Thing is, Father O'Neil used what he knew as leverage on me. There was another complaint, one Susan never knew about. From a parent in the Holy Cross congregation. It was the same old thing. O'Neil getting a crush on a younger member of the congregation. He had told an eighteen-year-old kid he was in love with him. O'Neil said if I helped him out he'd make sure what Susan did never came to light. So I spoke to the boy's parents. The boy had a charge for possession that was in the system. I got that disappeared and they dropped the complaint." Hennessy clutched Devlin's arm. "Please. Don't tell anyone what Susan did. She did it for honorable reasons. For her mother's condition. Please, Father. I know you're duty-bound to bring charges and I'll face the music. Just let us have a little time to... To prepare for what's to come."

"I'll see what I can do. Ted, I'm gonna ask one more time; do you think O'Neil killed the boys in the crypt and up on the hill?"

Hennessy scoffed. "No. No, physically he wasn't capable of swatting a fly. I don't know why Francis was going up to Oak Ridge like you say he was, but I can't believe that he had anything to do with murdering those boys. Like I told you, those dead boys are down to Driscoll and his brood. They're criminals, they're drug dealers, and I know they're murderers too. Or capable of it at least."

"It isn't Driscoll."

"You keep saying it isn't him but there's no other explanation. And that's not just me talking. it's what the Feds believe too. I don't know how you can be so damn sure it's not him."

"Because it doesn't make any sense, that's why. Yes, Driscoll is a thug, yes he's a criminal, but he's not stupid. He's not stupid enough to bury a body five hundred yards from where he's storing tens of thousands of dollars' worth of coke and MDMA. The guy runs a haulage firm, and his whole livelihood is based on transporting legal goods and illegal goods he doesn't want anyone to see in and out of Avery. He could easily have moved that body far away. He could have moved all the bodies far away. But instead, he buries one body in the old crypt and the other three boys on his own land. You tell me how that makes sense?"

"Because he's an arrogant son-of-a-bitch that's why. And it isn't anything to do with Francis. The thing about Francis was that he was a man ruled by pain. He was too full of his own pain to hurt anyone else. And that's the truth."

Devlin turned to look at Hennessy, his pleading eyes, the sweat on his forehead, and the spots of wine on his shirt. It was then that something broke in Devlin like a waterfall and all the small things he should have paid attention to came together. Suddenly he realized he had had the key to the deaths in Avery in his hand all along.

And that key was the word 'pain.'

34

T he Cardinal's residence was a large anonymous building. A huge, square-built brick structure. Inside though it was more like a small palace. Sarah followed a maid through a large vestibule leading to a larger lobby, off which branched various corridors and rooms. She waited in the lobby for a good ten minutes, not knowing quite why it was she was even there. Eventually, she heard footsteps approaching and turned to see a tall elderly man. His skin was dark and lined, and his eyes were deep-set.

"You must be Sarah?"

"Cardinal Hermes..."

"Father Devlin told me all about you. I'm so sorry about your brother."

"Thank you. I don't know why he asked me to come here..." A door shut behind her and she turned to see Father Devlin.

"Great, you're both here," said Devlin.

Hermes led Sarah and Devlin to an adjoining library room that smelled of old paper and dust. They sat facing each other at one of half a dozen desks

"So? Gabe? What is it? Why did you need to talk to us here?" asked Hermes

"Because I was wrong. I was wrong all along about something important. The drawing on the crypt ceiling above the body and on the tree bough in Oak Ridge, the image in your dreams, Sarah. It wasn't a tree of life or seven snakes. It was the image of a 'discipline.'"

"What's a discipline?" asked Sarah.

"It's a small whip used to self-inflict pain," replied Hermes "Flagellation. Also called mortification of the flesh. It's not a widespread practice but a few orders in the Catholic Church do still practice it. Using pain to make the soul pure."

"And that fired off a connection in my head I hadn't made," said Devlin. "But I should have. When I was at Father O'Neil's I found a spugna. A spugna is a small round disc embedded with pins that's used to strike against the chest to self-inflict pain. When I went to see Father Lopez he had a cilice in his study. A cilice is a chain worn around the thigh, also to self-inflict pain. Father Lopez was one of the people who reported one of the murdered boys as last being in Portland. Both Father O'Neil and Father Lopez practice mortification of the flesh."

"You think they're part of the same order?" asked Hermes.

"Yes. And the reason I asked to meet you both here is so we can check that in the Catholic Directory."

Hermes nodded, stood, and took two volumes from the library shelves. He placed them on the desk and pushed one of them toward Devlin.

"You look up Father O'Neil. I'll look up Father Lopez."

The two men flipped through pages and found the entries they were looking for.

"O'Neil was a member of the Order of Brothers in the Blood of Christ," said Devlin. "What about Lopez?"

"So is Lopez," confirmed Hermes. "The order runs a children's home not far from here. The Divine Mercy."

"I know that home," said Sarah. "It's has a private school and residential facility about halfway between Avery and Franklin. Do you think my brother Stephen and the other three boys were at that facility? That's why they ended up in Avery?"

"Yeah, that has to be what happened," said Devlin. "I'd bet my last dollar on it." Devlin pointed at the other Catholic Directories on the shelf. "Hector, could you check Father Deeney too."

"You think he's involved?" replied Hermes.

"Maybe."

Hermes took down another of the volumes of the Catholic Directory, laid it on the table, and flicked through to Deeney's entry.

"You're right, Gabe. He's a member of the order too. How did you know?"

"When I was talking to him at Holy Cross I noticed small dark spots on his tunic. And then, earlier today, I saw red spots on Hennessy's shirt too. At first, I thought it was wine or something else, but then it hit me. Those spots could be from using a spugna. That could cause small drops of blood to stain a shirt and tunic. And if there's a connection between O'Neil, Lopez, Deeney, and Hennessy, then that makes a cover-up of the boys' deaths a possibility."

"How would Hennessy be involved?" asked Hermes.

"The reports. All these people from different agencies providing reports the murdered boys were somewhere else, at least fifty miles away. What if all the people who have made reports to Hennessy have connections to The Divine Mercy or Brothers in the Blood of Christ? Ex-pupils, say. What if they and Hennessy have fabricated records putting the boys in other parts of the state? Away from Avery and away from The Divine Mercy. Hennessy would be the right person on the cops' side of thing to make that work, to sew that misinformation into the investigation. Make sure the investigation looked elsewhere and targeted Driscoll. Also, I know for certain now that Susan Hennessy has been skimming funds from the church. Ted Hennessy admitted that to me earlier today."

"He admitted it?" said Hermes astonished.

"Yeah. But the way he had it was that Susan was doing it without his knowledge in order to cover her mother's medical bills. He begged me to give him extra time before I did anything about it. But I'd bet it's all lies. I'd bet the money goes straight to the Brothers in the Blood of Christ."

"And maybe to the Divine Mercy," said Sarah.

"Why did Hennessy want extra time?" asked Hermes

"He said to get things between him and Susan in order. I think it's to buy him time to get ahead of the game somehow. What we don't know, though, is why those boys were killed. I have a strong suspicion there's a ceremonial aspect to the murders. The painting of the discipline and the same method of killing in each murder makes that likely to me."

"Sacrifice?" asked Sarah.

"Possibly. Maybe related to mortification of the flesh. I don't know for sure. We'd need to find out more somehow. About the Brothers in the Blood of Christ and The Divine Mercy."

"I can have the records for The Divine Mercy called up," said Hermes. "And see if the boys were registered there. Then I'll talk to the General Council about what we do next about the misallocation of funds at Holy Cross."

"Thanks, Hector. Why don't you and I make a visit to The Divine Mercy?" Devlin said to Sarah. "See exactly what kind of place your brother ended up at."

35

Sarah made arrangements to cover her morning classes, and she and Devlin set off early the next day to visit The Divine Mercy School. It was a five-minute drive from the i-495. The sign for the home, a big white board with the name painted in red letters, stood on the grass verge and in front of a gray wooden building. A smaller road led off along the side of the building up to a cluster of similar structures. The whole site was set on acres and acres of green. But the feature of The Divine Mercy Children's home that was most striking was the high chain-link fence topped with barbed wire that ran along the entire perimeter of the compound. It transformed the character of the home into something more akin to a minimum-security prison.

They parked by the gates. A delivery truck was turning into the main entrance and electric gates whirred open to let it in. Devlin and Sarah got out of the car and followed behind the truck, which stopped abruptly. The driver poked his head out of the cab and shouted back at them over the running engine.

"Hey... I'm not supposed to let anyone else in."

Devlin approached the driver who by now had noticed his clerical collar.

"Oh, hi, Father. I didn't see you were a priest."

"That's okay. We're expected."

"No problem," said the driver, saluting with two fingers.

The driver drove on into the compound. Devlin and Sarah headed for the building at the front of the complex, which looked like the reception.

Inside the building was a lobby and a front desk. Behind the desk was an office, but no staff. Devlin hit the bell on the desk and they waited. After a full minute a nun appeared from a side room and approached the desk. She looked at both Sarah and Devlin in turn, though she lingered on Devlin.

"Hello, Father Devlin."

"Hello, sister. Have we met?"

"No. But I saw you speak at a fundraiser a couple of weeks ago. How did you get in through the gate?"

"Oh, we followed a delivery truck in."

"Did you have an appointment to see someone? Visits here are strictly by appointment."

"We didn't make an appointment, Sister...? I'm sorry, I don't know your name."

"Maureen. Sister Maureen." Sister Maureen looked for a moment as if she were going to reprimand Devlin, but then her expression suddenly softened. "I'm so sorry about Father O'Neil."

"Thank you. It's just a terrible business and awful for his sister."

"Yes. I can't imagine." Sister Maureen smiled sympathetically. "What can I do for you, Father? Who is it you wanted to see?"

"We weren't here to see anyone in particular." Devlin gestured to Sarah. "This is Sarah Wilson, a congregant of mine. I'm here with Sarah in the hope we might find some information."

"What kind of information?"

"Sarah here is looking for her adopted brother and someone in the family had heard that he'd spent some time at The Divine Mercy."

Sister Maureen gave another sympathetic look. "I'm afraid I can't divulge details about our past students. You'd need to make an official request in writing."

"Okay," said Sarah. "I'll do that."

"If you hold on, I'll give you the email address for our records department." Sister Maureen disappeared and then came back with a folded note and handed it to Sarah.

"Thanks, Sister, appreciate it."

"No problem at all. I hope you find your brother."

"I hope so too. Thanks for your help."

Sarah and Devlin came back out into the hard sunlight and cold morning air. Sarah reached into her pocket, pulled out her cell, and started typing.

"What are you doing?"

"I'm putting in that written request right now."

"Once you've done that do you feel like a walk?"

"Where to?"

Devlin looked along the road that led to the little village of gray-painted wooden houses scattered around.

"Now we're in, we shouldn't waste the opportunity. Let's take the tour."

Strolling casually, as if they were sightseers in a foreign town, they followed the single road that led into the center of the complex. Walking between the houses, they peered in at the windows and detoured off the road and into the areas behind. Here they found basketball and soccer courts. There were huts too that looked temporary and less attractive than the neat little buildings out front.

As they had walked, every so often, through the front

windows of the houses, Devlin and Sarah would catch sight of a small group of children sitting around a table. Each of these wooden houses was a classroom and right now the children in the houses were in the middle of a morning session.

Suddenly a bell rang out across this strange, eerily silent campus and doors to the buildings and huts opened. Men in habits, brothers of a religious order, emerged from the classrooms and behind them followed lines of silent, sullen kids in their early to mid-teens. The kids had exercise books gripped in their hands and school bags over their shoulders. In a matter of minutes, there were dozens of lines of students crisscrossing the grounds following their brother. Each line trailed along the road to another house that had just been emptied of its students, swapping over classrooms, with the brothers keeping a close eye on their charges.

During this mass changeover, Devlin and Sarah had kept walking. They left the wooden houses, huts and the children behind them, and the road they were on became much steeper. Ahead of them, in the distance and higher up, they could see a high brick wall covered in creepers and an open iron gate. As they got closer they glimpsed a large brick house that lay behind the walls. This brick house was substantially more impressive than the wooden buildings it overlooked. The road came to an end at the iron gate and turned into a graveled path.

"Look at that," said Sarah, pointing up at the house. "The carved stone in the middle."

Above the main door of the house was a square stone plaque. Carved on the plaque was a relief sculpture of a lamb curled up as if sleeping. Below it, also carved, were the words, *'Dolor sit radix amoris.'*

"Hey..."

The shout came from behind. Devlin and Sarah turned to

see a man in the distance walking toward them. He was tall, and dressed in a cassock and a clerical collar.

"I guess the game's up. What do we do?" asked Sarah.

"We do nothing. We just see where this goes."

Devlin and Sarah waited for the man who was climbing the hill.

"It's Father Lopez," said Devlin.

"Who?"

"The Greenfield priest who said he reported one of the murdered boys to the social services."

"He must work here. That makes sense."

Lopez was striding toward them now, making quick work of the steep gradient and looking furious.

"Father Devlin. What are you doing here?"

"We were just taking a look around," Devlin replied. "This is a friend of mine, Sarah. She's a teacher so she was interested to see the home and its educational provision. That's okay, isn't it?"

"No. Of course it's not okay. You need to call ahead. To make an appointment. We need to know at all times who is here. We can't have strangers coming in and out of the home. Our job is to protect the children."

"Of course. You're right. I should have realized. I'm sorry. I guess you work here too?"

"Yes. I teach the boys physical education. Now, I need to escort you back to the entrance. If you want to visit, please arrange it through the office."

"What's this building?" asked Sarah pointing to the brick mansion behind them. "It's older than the rest of the compound."

"That's the residence of the order of brothers who teach here. Now, please, follow me."

Devlin and Sarah walked with Lopez back down the hill.

"Father Lopez," said Sarah. "My brother attended The Divine Mercy. His name was Stephen Martin. Do you remember him?"

"No," replied Lopez almost immediately. "I don't recall that name. I'm sorry."

"It seems quite an austere set up here," noted Devlin.

"It is intended to be a very strict regime. The children we accept here have been excluded from society, neglected, turned away from every other place. They are the most challenging students. But The Divine Mercy has an outstanding reputation for turning those children around. Our students have gone on to work in many distinguished fields and risen to very high places indeed. Far beyond their early circumstances. We have many ex-students that have gone on to be top lawyers and even senators."

"Really?"

"Really."

"The security here's quite something."

"We take the children's safety seriously, Father. It's the priority here."

"Safety?" Devlin nodded and looked around the campus. "You know, some might say all these apparatus looks like it's there to keep the children in."

"It's there to keep them safe."

Lopez left them outside the front gates and walked back to the reception. The high electric gates shut behind him.

"The inscription on the Brothers' residence said '*Dolor sit radix amoris,*'" said Devlin. "It means, 'Pain is the root of love.' It's a variation of a quote extolling the mortification of the flesh. I'd say The Brothers in the Blood of Christ are definitely ritual practitioners. That ties back to the paintings of the discipline and maybe the ritual aspect to the murders."

"That's the place," said Sarah with complete conviction. "That's where my brother was. Where he was killed. I can feel it in my blood."

"I believe you. But we have to get proof. We need Cardinal Hermes to come through with the records and prove the boys went here. I rang first thing, but he still hasn't got them. As soon as we get the records we'll have something solid enough to go straight to the Feds with."

36

After Devlin had dropped Sarah at school he drove into Avery to run a few errands and pick up supplies. As he was pulling out of the strip mall parking lot he glimpsed the headlights of a black Mercedes in his rearview mirror; the same Mercedes that had tailed him two nights before. He traveled a couple of blocks till he hit the edge of town and checked his mirror again. The Mercedes was still there and now not even hiding the fact it was tailing Devlin.

Devlin got onto the turnpike heading for Holy Cross and heard an engine rev from behind. The Mercedes was gathering speed and moving up close to Devlin's bumper. Then suddenly it moved out into the next lane, overtook, and power-slid to a stop where it straddled the road, causing Devlin to emergency brake and squeal to a halt only a few feet away.

The door of the Mercedes opened and Tony Driscoll got out. He moved with a slight limp, a sobering reminder of their last encounter. Devlin got out too.

"Why have you been tailing me?" said Devlin. "It was you following me from Greenfield last night. If you want to have it out with me just walk up to me and have it out."

"You're being tailed because you messed with the wrong family, Devlin. For as long as you're in Avery the Driscolls will be keeping an eye on you. But I'm here to tell you something else too. It's not me."

"WHAT'S NOT YOU?"

"The four boys. They're nothing to do with me. That fat sonofabitch Hennessy is trying to hang it on me."

"The tunnel under the tomb, though. That's yours, isn't it?"

"Of course it's damn well mine. But I had nothing to do with those boys, and neither did any other Driscoll."

"Why are you telling me?"

"Because you think you know it all and really you know less than nothing. Because you're the priest at Holy Cross and you need to know that O'Neil was in on it. In on it all. And that's why he's dead. And that's what you've inherited. It's all on you, pal."

"What was O'Neil in on?"

Driscoll hovered for a moment, seemingly about to say more. Then abruptly he got in his car and sped off.

Devlin spent his journey back thinking about what Driscoll had said. As soon as he got back to the rectory he'd get hold of Driscoll's address and go see him. Then he'd do whatever he had to do to extract more information out of him.

He pulled into the drive in front of the rectory and checked his watch. It was mid-afternoon and he still hadn't heard back from Hermes about The Divine Mercy records. Devlin glanced at his cell and saw a missed call from the Bishop's office. No doubt they wanted a conversation about the timing of his replacement. There was also a text from Sarah asking him to call her and also, at last, a voicemail from Hermes. He dialed into his voicemail and listened to Hermes's message. The signal came and went but he managed to make out that Hermes had drawn a blank. The four murdered boys weren't on The Divine Mercy's records.

For a few minutes, Devlin stood completely immersed in thought. Hermes's message had completely thrown him. It was impossible, thought Devlin, that the boys hadn't been at The Divine Mercy. It made complete sense. It was a home for vulnerable and homeless children. Exactly the kind of victims they had found buried in Avery.

Then a possible explanation hit him. Because The Divine Mercy was an independently run religious children's home, it might hold all of its students' records separately. In which case they could doctor it how they liked.

If that was the case then what Devlin needed was an independent record of students at The Divine Mercy. He called Hermes but got no answer. Then he typed out a short text and pressed send. The signal was playing up again he so held his cell up to catch some bars and pressed send again. Before he could check if the text had been sent a sickening thud spread like lightning through his head. His cell fell out of his hand, and as the side of his face hit the graveled ground he was dimly aware of voices. And then the voices stopped.

37

The room didn't have any windows. Just one single bulb hung from the ceiling. Every so often there was a buzzing sound and the bulb flickered off and on, briefly throwing the room into complete darkness. The only furniture was a mattress on the floor, a chair against the wall, a sink by the door, and a metal pot in the corner. A crucifix was screwed into the wall above the bed. On the chair were folded black robes.

It was deathly quiet. Wherever he was it was far away from the outside. He had no idea how long he'd been waiting for. At a guess, a couple of hours.

His ears pricked up at the sound of distant steps. The steps got louder and closer until they stopped outside the door. Keys jangled, the lock turned, and the door opened.

In stepped a tall, athletic man in a monk's habit and leather sandals.

"Jamie. I'm so glad you came back."

Jamie was crouched on the mattress, his knees pulled close to his body.

"I didn't come back, Father Deeney. I was kidnapped. That's illegal."

"We had to come find you. I really believe we had no other choice. You knew there was more work to do with you. To cure you."

"I don't need curing."

Father Deeney sat on the end of the mattress, placing his hands on the soft surface, spreading out his long fingers. Jamie instinctively pulled back from him. Deeney looked at Jamie for a long while before he spoke.

"There is something inside of you, Jamie. Something dark and not within your control."

A tear rolled from Jamie's eye.

"You are so fortunate," continued Deeney softly, "that I can see the things that lie within people, the forces that trouble them. You are a very troubled student Jamie. You caused so much trouble."

"I'm so sorry, Father. I didn't mean to be so bad. I'll be better. I swear."

"I know you will. Because I'm going to make you better. Whatever it takes." Deeney pointed a finger at Jamie and then pushed it into his chest. Where Deeney touched him Jamie felt as if his skin was burning. "You will thank me."

Deeney stood and smiled down at Jamie, whose eyes were brimming with tears.

"Let me go, please. Let me go."

"I will. I promise you, I will. Now, change into the clothes provided for you and I'll be back."

Deeney left and Jamie looked over at the robes folded on the chair. It was a black habit. He stood, undid his shirt and, in the place where Deeney had touched him, he saw the skin was red and blistered.

38

Devlin hadn't replied to any of Sarah's calls or texts, so first thing she headed around to Holy Cross and knocked on the rectory door. Devlin didn't answer so she went around the front of the church. Nobody was about. She tried the church hall on the other side of the grounds but that was locked. So, she gave up and drove to school to prepare for classes.

Throughout the day she called and left messages but got no answer. Then, after she'd finished her last class and done a round of marking, she drove back over to Holy Cross. This time there were people about.

Tanner, the sexton, was talking to Susan Hennessy outside the rectory.

She approached them and asked, "Is Father Devlin around?"

Susan Hennessy glanced at Tanner, who answered.

"I'm afraid not."

"Do you know where he is? I haven't been able to contact him all day."

"None of us have," said Susan. "He's missed Mass, two meetings, and confessionals. No one's heard a word from him. Except for the text he sent me."

"What did the text say?"

"That he'd been called out of town for a few days on urgent business. But that was it. Nothing else."

"That's really odd."

"I honestly am not surprised," replied Susan. "He is just not cut out to be a priest. He's too... unorthodox. And that's putting it politely."

Then Susan Hennessy marched off, leaving Tanner and Sarah standing in an uncomfortable silence.

"It is strange," said Tanner.

"He didn't say anything to you?"

"Nothing."

"It's not right. I need to go see the Cardinal."

FOR THE SECOND time in two days, Sarah called on Cardinal Hermes. The maid went to fetch the Cardinal while Sarah waited in the lobby area admiring large oil paintings of previous Cardinals set in gilt frames.

"Miss Wilson." Cardinal Hermes appeared at one of the entrances to the lobby.

"Cardinal. Thank you for seeing me at such short notice."

"Please, come with me."

Hermes led Sarah to the library.

"You said it was about Father Devlin?"

"Yes. I can't get hold of him and he hasn't been at the church."

"I called Holy Cross myself. I've been told he left a message saying he'll be out of town?"

"Well, yeah, but that's kind of weird isn't it?"

"It is. I've been trying to get hold of him all day myself. I've got the student records for The Divine Mercy."

"And?"

"The names of the four boys aren't on there."

"That can't be."

"That's what Father Devlin thought too. He sent me a text saying he thought we couldn't trust the Divine Mercy's records. That we need other more reliable records."

"Like what?"

"Well, he suggested the immunization records. And it worked. The Diocese keeps those records centrally for all religious schools and shares them with the State Education Department. All four boys received vaccines and all four are down as attending The Divine Mercy."

"I knew it. So, what should we do now?"

"We should go to the police."

Sarah thought for a moment and then said, decisively, "No. Father Devlin didn't trust Avery P.D."

"Then what do you suggest?"

"He said to go straight to the Feds. That's what we should do."

39

H e had no watch and no window. No sense at all of how much time was passing. It was deathly quiet too and had been for almost the entire time he'd been locked up. At one point he heard footsteps along the hallway, and a door opening. Not long after, he heard the door shut, then footsteps passed back down the hallway and faded away to silence.

Jamie lived in fear of two things; no one coming for him and someone coming for him. And eventually, someone had to come for him. He knew that. He knew the man who ran this place was as hard as nails and capable of anything.

So, when the footsteps came again he crawled onto the mattress and backed into the corner of the room. Fear erupted from deep within him and possessed him entirely. The footsteps stopped outside the door, a key turned in the lock, and the door opened.

Father Deeney and another man that Jamie didn't recognize stepped into the room. He was short, broad, and overweight, and held a gold chalice. They both wore hooded robes and brown leather belts with a small scabbard attached.

"It's time, Jamie," said Deeney.

"Time for what?"

"Time to make you well. To cure you."

"I don't want to be cured."

Deeney sighed. "I wish we could trust what you say, Jamie. But they are the words of the demon inside you. The demon that has taken hold of you. You no more know what's good for you than Satan himself."

"I don't have a demon inside of me."

Deeney shut his eyes and closed his hands into fists. He opened his eyes wide and breathed in and out slowly. "We did try with you, Jamie. Tried so hard. We showed you so much patience. But the way you behaved. The vandalism, the violence to others, the drugs, the stealing. We warned you so many times. But you thought until the very end that you could escape the consequences of what you have done."

Jamie couldn't help thinking that Deeney was right. That he had done all of those things, and more. He might even have killed a man. That maybe he deserved everything that was coming to him.

Deeney stepped forward and crouched by the mattress. Jamie pressed his back hard up against where the two walls met and made himself as small as he could.

"But it isn't your fault," Deeney whispered. "None of this is your fault. And what happens next will not be your fault." Deeney took Jamie's face in his hands, cradling him gently. "Some people are just destined to fall foul of the devil. There is a serpent inside you. Wriggling around and slithering into every wicked thought you have. But I am not afraid of this serpent because I have faith. Complete faith. Faith that I am the man who has been sent to free you."

Deeney stood. "Now, first you will need to drink."

The man holding the gold chalice stepped forward.

"What if I refuse?" said Jamie.

"It will make no difference. In the end."

40

Devlin felt sick and cold. His ankles and wrists had been bound by thick rope in a handcuff knot. He was sitting on a long narrow bench that sat up against one side of the room. A large crucifix hung on the wall, below which was a chair. Apart from the bench, that was the only other piece of furniture in a brick-walled room that measured about ten by ten. *It must have been a boiler room at one time,* thought Devlin. Dirty metal pipes still ran along the sides of the wall but were empty and silent, and no longer fed the building above with warmth. He had no recollection of anything following the blow to his head, and suspected he'd been drugged to keep him under.

Draped on the back of the chair were clothes. Dark robes that looked like a monk's habit.

Devlin stood, waited for the wooziness to wear off a little, and picked up the habit.

It was a plain black robe except for a symbol that had been sewn into the breast. The symbol was a discipline, seven ropes of a whip, just like the symbol on the ceiling of the crypt and the tree in Oak Ridge.

Footsteps echoed down the corridor. They grew louder until they stopped outside the room. The door opened and Father Deeney and Detective Hennessy entered. Both were dressed in the same black habits decorated with the discipline.

"Hello, Father Devlin," said Deeney, smiling.

"Really?" said Devlin, indicating his roped hands and feet.

"I think it's for the best."

"Ted," said Devlin, "I can't say I'm surprised."

"You really made life difficult for me, Father," Ted replied. "But you're finding out what you should have known all along. That I run this town, not you."

"I do blame myself," said Devlin. "It was all there and I should have seen it sooner. The connection between the first body with the whip on the ceiling, Father O'Neil, Lopez, you, Hennessy. This is a cult. A cult based on the mortification of the flesh. Punishing the body to save the soul. Except you took it so much further. I think you believe there are some people for whom pain isn't enough. Suffering will not give them redemption. Only complete annihilation of the flesh will deliver their soul."

Deeney nodded. "And I think you put it all together because you recognize how far gone your own soul is. How entwined with sin you are. How similarly desperate the remedy must be for you."

Devlin looked at Hennessy, who was holding a short stick, and shook his head.

"You really believe all of this too, Ted? You were involved in the murder of those boys? All four of those poor souls murdered, buried without ceremony in a shallow grave."

"They had ceremony," Deeney replied. "We gave them all the ceremony they could want. And they weren't poor souls. They were deeply troubled souls." He shook his head and tutted. "Souls that might not have been saved, had it not been for me.

The Divine Mercy Children's Home is so much more than just a children's home. Miraculous transformations happen here. We take those without hope, without anything at all, and turn them into God-fearing citizens. Into lawyers, doctors, police commissioners, DAs, senators. And moreover, we turn them into loyal soldiers to our cause. However, there are some who come to us that, after great heartache and struggle, we understand cannot be saved in this world.

"You see, we don't allow sin to infect our corner of the world. We simply won't permit disobedience, self-indulgence, or lack of discipline. We forbid it. Because what others describe as the ills of society, the poison of individualism, we see for what these things are: demons. From time to time a boy has come through this place and they have bridled and bucked against our teachings. Rebelled. Like Lucifer himself. And no amount of discipline, no matter how instructional, will bring them to heel. In these boys, this select few, I began to understand something was festering, something far worse than mere insubordination. That they were at the mercy of evil spirits. And that these cases of possession were so dreadful that no punishment, no matter how extreme, could be worse than the cause. I have been able to free these boys."

"By strangling them?"

"By releasing them. And I have also become very experienced in diagnosing these cases in earlier stages. Before it has a chance to spread, infect, and damage others. Indeed, you might say I have a sixth sense for it. And when I first met you, Father Devlin, I sensed immediately that there was something very special about you. I instinctively sensed a familiar force within you, an evil spirit working in your heart and mind, running through your blood, that had corrupted you entirely."

Deeney leaned in toward Devlin. "There is a demon inside

you. I don't know how it got there but it's there. You know it too. But you are very lucky, Father. I am the man who will set you free. It was destiny that we meet."

"You going to strangle me too?"

"I am going to release you. If that means you die, well, better you are clean to be received into heaven than live the rest of your life bound to a demon and plunged into hell for an eternity."

"I suppose when you put it like that I should be grateful. And Father O'Neil. Why did he have to die?"

"Father O'Neil was about to go to the police. Tell them everything. Because of you."

"Me?"

"He was terrified of you. He thought you were some kind of avenging demon sent by God come to punish him for his sins. He was losing his sanity, frankly, visiting the graves of the boys at all hours, painting trees. I'm sure cancer and guilt were also contributing to his unhinged state of mind. Alas, Francis was not without sin, I'm afraid. So out of compassion I swapped out some of his meds for sleeping pills and eased him out of his troubled life. He is in a much more peaceful place now."

"He had something to do with the first boy, didn't he? The one in the old crypt. Stephen."

"Father O'Neil was heavily involved in the way of our spiritual teachings here at the home. But he also had his own struggles. He struggled with... feelings... urges, you might say. It was his personal cross. And he struggled with his feelings for Stephen. When I told Father O'Neil my plans for Stephen, that we had come to the end of the road with the boy, O'Neil couldn't hide his feelings anymore. He tried to stop me, and when it became clear that was not possible he asked, begged actually, that Stephen be buried on consecrated ground.

"I agreed to make the old crypt the boy's final resting place.

Father O'Neil painted the discipline on the crypt wall to secretly mark the exact spot of Stephen's grave, where his head lay. So he could visit it, pay his respects from time to time." Deeney paused, exchanged glances with Hennessy, and then continued, "I have another tormented soul to care for. Then we will be back for you. Hennessy here has requested some private time with you. Apparently, there is some outstanding business between you two."

Deeney left. Hennessy waited, closing and locking the door behind them. He turned to Devlin.

"Ever since you came to Avery, Father, you have caused me headache after goddamned headache. Tormenting me, my wife, and Father O'Neil. Good people trying to do their best in a bad world. You really are a dreadful man."

"Y'know, there are a lot of people who would agree with you, Ted. You took the money from Holy Cross for the Order, didn't you, Ted? You, Susan, and Father O'Neil."

"We took it for something we believe in. This place is the only answer for so many boys." Hennessy tapped the stick he was carrying against his palm. "I made up the story about Susan's mom to buy us some time. So we could find a way of rounding you up and taking you out of the picture. And now we have, I intend to inflict suffering on your flesh to atone for your wretched soul."

"Any chance you could undo these ropes? Make it something like a fair contest?"

"I'll let you stand up. How's that?"

"That's very sporting of you."

Devlin stood. He still felt weak and not quite steady on his feet. Whatever drug they'd given him, some of it was still in his system. Hennessy flicked his wrist and the short stick in his hand snapped out into a baton.

"Right," said Devlin. "I see how this is going down..."

Hennessy swung a vicious backhand, whipping the baton towards the side of Devlin's head. Devlin instinctively raised his shoulder and the stick bounced off his upper arm and clipped the side of his head. Devlin retreated to make space. Hennessy seemed to have transformed into a different man. He had a wild look in his eyes and Devlin sensed an onslaught coming. He lurched at Devlin again, raining down blows. Devlin did as much as he could to dodge and slip the strikes of the baton, but he was a big man in a small space unable to move or hit back. He was an easy target and Hennessy was like a man possessed.

Devlin turned to the brick wall and hunched up for protection. A hard whip of metal exploded into his kidney and he thought his insides were going to burst. There was nowhere to go as he felt frenzied blows shudder through his body.

Hennessy badly wanted Devlin to go down. To hit the floor like a cowering animal, and although Devlin felt the strength draining from him, he refused. Pushed up against the wall, feeling like this flogging was never going to end, Devlin's hands felt an object, something cold and hard. Instinctively he pulled at it, wrenching it away from the wall, and swung it as hard as he could as if he were blistering a ball for a home run. The end of the object connected with its target and Devlin felt the violence of the blow, skull-cracking, and skin lacerating with the might of it.

Hennessy was on the floor, the side of his head bleeding. Devlin knelt and found a pulse. It was only then he saw what he was holding in his hand and what had caused Hennessy so much pain. It was the iron crucifix on the wall.

Devlin used the knife from Hennessy's belt to cut away the ropes. Then he found the keys to the door in the pocket of Hennessy's robes and locked the man up. Devlin left him unconscious on the floor, the soon-to-be recipient of a holy headache.

Devlin was soon out in a hallway made of stone walls and

concrete floors, and lit by a couple of naked bulbs hanging from the ceiling. He paused, trying to work out where he should go next, and which way he should turn in this strange dungeon.

The three men formed a triangle around him and led him further into the bowels of the building. One brother behind him, and two in front holding flaming torches. Jamie recognized the brother following him but did not know his name. He'd seen him at morning Mass at The Divine Mercy and around the compound. But he hadn't taught him, and he wasn't one of the brothers who had routinely beaten him. Jamie figured he must be part of Deeney's inner circle; the ones who knew what really happened here.

Deeney was in front. Jamie also recognized the brother beside him. He was Father Lopez, who had taught him physical education and once given him a particularly savage beating in private. All the more savage because of the pleasure he seemed to take from it.

Nobody spoke. As they traveled further along the dark, damp tunnel, the walls and ceiling began to taper in. Jamie became gripped by claustrophobia as he felt his own space and time begin to converge to a final terrifying point. It was clear to the boy that any destination this far away from the world above was one from which he would not return.

Jamie began to sob and the sobbing quickly grew out of control into a full-blown panic attack. He felt the bodies around him close in, and arms grab and restrain his twisting, flailing body until finally, despite his desperate wails, he was being carried along gasping for breath, his feet dragging along the floor.

The tunnel stopped at an iron door which Deeney pushed open. Beyond the door was a cave illuminated by candles laid out in a circle on the floor and along the rocky ledges. Four more brothers in robes were standing silently in a cross formation around the edge of the cave.

No attempt had been made to turn this place into a habitable space; it was stark, hard, and jagged. The roof of the cave curved like a crude vaulted ceiling and was covered with stalactites. Dark voids in the walls hinted at smaller tunnels leading to other even more remote caves. The only embellishment in this cavern was the figure of a lamb drawn in white paint on the floor. In the middle of the cave, bolted to the uneven floor, was a large, rectangular table with leather restraining cuffs. Jamie noticed that the table, made out of thick unvarnished wood, was stained with dark brown patches.

Suddenly and with overwhelming force, the brothers lifted Jamie and carried him to the table where they laid him down and secured the cuffs around his wrists, ankles, and neck. He was bound so tightly that movement was impossible. He lay, panting, forced to look directly upwards. In this position, Jamie could only see the cave ceiling above. In the center of the ceiling and directly above him was a black hole, like a chimney, and from it he felt a faint breeze of cold air.

Deeney noticed that Jamie was staring at the small black hole. He whispered, "That is the only way out of here for you, Jamie. Ascension upwards, through the earth toward heaven."

He leaned over Jamie and cupped his face.

"What are you going to do with me?" asked Jamie in a whisper.

"Save you, Jamie. We must save you. We have no choice. It's why I came to get you. Hunted you down. There is a demon inside you and we must operate on you to take it out. And then we must extinguish it."

"Will it hurt?"

"Yes, Jamie. It will hurt."

"Are you going to kill me?"

"No. No, I'm not going to kill you."

Jamie sighed with relief.

"I will send you to live in eternity with your Lord."

Jamie began to scream but Deeney seemed to know this was about to happen and covered his mouth with duct tape. Then he stepped away. Jamie smelled incense filling the cold, open space. The seven brothers began to chant in Latin and their voices slowly grew louder. As the voices rose in volume Jamie felt a pinpoint of heat in his chest exactly where Deeney had touched him earlier. The heat began to grow in size and intensity, as if an invisible red-hot arrow was piercing him.

Deeney returned and stood over him. He seemed to know that this strange heat was inside him and he placed his hand on Jamie's chest precisely at the center of the sensation. But his hand made the heat stronger, hotter, and desperately uncomfortable. The heat began to spread until Jamie started to feel like his internal organs were on fire. And even more strangely, he felt the heat become a thing, a thing inside him with its own agency, battling and squirming against Deeney's touch.

The chanting had now broken into shouting. It was the same Latin phrases but yelled and in some cases screamed as the surrounding circle of brothers reached a frenzy. Jamie looked to his right and saw that the brothers were in some kind of blind ecstasy. Deeney seemed unmoved by the noise around him, remaining the calm in the center of the storm.

"This demon will not leave your mortal body, Jamie," said Deeney. He was holding a thin silver blade which he raised and held over Jamie's heart. Jamie screamed through his bandaged mouth and arced and twisted against his restraints. Yet, nothing he could do could stop the events that had been put in motion. His body felt like a kiln pounding out heat, sweat pouring off every inch of his skin.

And what was inside him? What was this thing wriggling and struggling like a small animal trapped in a bag?

Deeney was now intoning in English. "May God arise, may his enemies be scattered; may his foes flee before him. As smoke is blown away by the wind, may you blow them away; as wax melts before the fire, may the wicked perish before God. But may the righteous be glad and rejoice before God; may they be happy and joyful."

He took the collar of Jamie's robe and began cutting through the material with his knife. He severed the cloth down to the navel and opened up the robe to expose Jamie's naked chest.

42

D evlin had chosen to follow the tunnel down into darkness. Deeper, down into the bowels of the building and away from the thin light of the bulbs that lit the higher parts of the tunnel.

The further Devlin went the blacker it became. He felt the downward slant of the floor underfoot and the walls on either side coming closer together. Eventually, it was so dark he couldn't see his hand in front of his face, let alone the path in front of him. He heard tiny feet scratch against the stone floor as rats crisscrossed the tunnel, their bodies scrambling over his feet. He was starting to convince himself that he'd made the wrong decision about which way to go, when he heard something up ahead that chilled his flesh. It was the sound of frenzied screaming and wailing, part human, part animal, part chanting, part wailing. Grabbing at the walls to feel his way forward he began to hurry faster, as fast as he dared in the dark. A few times his foot hit a bump in the increasingly uneven floor and he tumbled forward, the rats fleeing from his falling bulk. But the wails and screams were getting louder and finally he came up against a dead-end. His hands made out the frame of a solid iron door from behind which the cries were coming. He pushed hard against the door and it scraped open, revealing a torch and candle-lit catacomb.

43

D evlin counted seven men in the cave and in the center was a boy strapped to a table. The men were dressed in habits and in various states of wild frenzy. Father Deeney was standing by the table, leaning over the boy, his eyes wide and possessed. He had marked out a cross on the boy's chest with a knife and blood was dripping down his sides, along the grooves of the boy's rib cage and onto the table beneath him. Deeney placed the knife on the table, pulled up the sleeves of his habit, and wrapped his hands around the boy's neck.

Devlin rushed toward Deeney, grabbed his arm, and yanked him around. Seeing Devlin seemed to snap Deeney out of his trance. He clutched the dagger from the table, but before he could use it Devlin socked him hard, jabbing straight into the bridge of his nose, sending him backward onto the floor.

The brothers were still wailing and keening, unaware of what was happening in front of them. Quickly Devlin set about undoing Jamie's straps, wrapping his torn robe back around him, and sitting him upright. The boy's eyes were dilated, as if he were drugged. His face was chalk white, his neck was red, and his body was covered in his own blood.

"I'm here to help you," said Devlin. "What's your name?"

The boy didn't answer. Instead, he shivered for a moment, then finally muttered, "They're going to kill me..." He was drugged and so deep in shock that he couldn't even feel the cuts that Deeney had inflicted on him.

Devlin didn't have time to reply. He realized that the chanting was subsiding and starting to trail away. Deeney was still laid out on the ground but the other six robed figures encircling the table were coming round from their trance and staring at Devlin and the now freed boy. Confusion was turning into startled outrage. Devlin recognized one of the men as Father Lopez.

"Devlin?" Lopez stepped forward, not hiding his aggression. "You are not permitted here. You are trespassing."

Devlin squared up. "You're not laying another finger on the kid."

"There is no way you can get out of here," said Lopez. "You're as trapped and helpless as the boy you vainly want to protect."

Devlin took another look around and assessed the situation. Deeney was still out cold. Intuition and experience told him that of the other six men Lopez posed the main threat. Two of the men looked like they could handle themselves okay and were strong enough to be a concern. Yet he was pretty sure those two would wait on how things played out with Lopez first. The other three didn't look as if they'd ever had a fight in their life. He was betting they'd react like most other people; they would either freeze, or fold quickly in the face of real violence.

Lopez took another step toward Devlin, now only a yard away. The boy had slid under the table and was curled into a shivering ball.

"I told you," said Devlin, "you're not coming near this boy."

"You won't be able to stop me."

"If you get past me — if — I'll have done so much damage

you won't be able to walk out of here."

Lopez smiled and had the look of a man who had no doubt he would win. "I'm younger, I'm faster. I enjoy pain. I have the edge."

Devlin knew Lopez was right. He was in peak physical shape and sharp as a tack. In other situations, Devlin might have let Lopez make the first move. Not this time. He was too cocky and too good. So, Devlin backed off a little to invite Lopez in. Lopez took the bait and once he was close enough Devlin let off a hook. Lopez saw it coming and hacked it away with the blade of his hand. He didn't see the follow-up; Devlin's devastating kick to his knee. Pain blew up in his joint and he retreated a pace. Devlin looked around once more. The two other possible contenders had also stepped back and down, keeping their powder dry.

"An old man's trick," said Lopez, limping.

"Yeah, funny, I find it works on young men best of all."

Lopez came back at Devlin with speed and force, unleashing a flurry of mixed martial arts blows that were astonishingly quick, neat, and deadly. Devlin's mind went blank and a mixture of his training and instinctive reactions took over. He matched each blow, blocking and parrying, but fast as he was Lopez, was faster. Two blows got through, a strike to the face and one into his side.

Devlin took a breath, planted his feet, and went for round two. Again, Lopez came at him with a flurry of precise, lethal blows, punches, and kicks. Devlin engaged head-on, defensive but pushing forward and with sheer determination, he ran Lopez back. It even seemed like he was tipping the balance when, out of nowhere, Lopez pulled out a roundhouse kick. The contact couldn't have been more perfect and for a moment, on the way to the ground, the world went black.

Then Devlin was awake again but now on his back. He was

suddenly aware of someone beside him. It was the bloodied, pathetic figure of Jamie, hugging his knees under the table. Immediately Devlin rolled hard to his left, missing the heel of Lopez's foot. He swung up and around to standing, and summoned every fiber of energy and strength he had left.

It was on again, another relentless flurry of blows and kicks from Lopez. Lopez was faster and fitter, and Devlin realized he had to use the one thing he had to his advantage. Strength. He plowed head-on into the blows, parrying and blocking, pushing Lopez back. But this time he picked up speed, bent low, and lunged into Lopez's midriff. Pounding fists and kicks rained on Devlin's body but it was too late. Devlin had Lopez in his grip and lifted him over his head. Skinny and taught in build, he must have weighed little more than a hundred and sixty pounds wringing wet. And now he was in Devlin's world.

In one mighty overhead throw, Devlin hurled Lopez hard as he could against the craggy, rough-hewn cave wall. Lopez dropped onto the floor, nearly broken by the collision. Devlin didn't waste any time and lashed out at Lopez, kicking him till he rolled over onto his back, now barely conscious.

"Lookout..." The voice was high and feminine. Devlin turned to see Jamie screaming at him. But Devlin only understood what he was screaming about too late. He felt the searing pain of a blade in his back. With great difficulty, he turned to see Deeney holding his bloody knife and glaring at Devlin. His eyes were red and full of hate.

"Time to release you too, Father Devlin."

Deeney thrust the knife into Devlin again and pulled it out. Devlin staggered back.

The knife must have gone in deep because Devlin could feel his legs go beneath him. His pararescue training told him a major internal artery had most likely been ruptured. That meant major internal bleeding. He realized he probably didn't have long to live. Then he revised his diagnosis from probably to definitely.

Devlin dropped to one knee. He could feel it, feel life draining from him. Even now he was very likely beyond medical help. Beyond any earthly help. Death, Devlin reflected, wasn't like in the movies. In real life, you could taste it, smell it.

Deeney had crouched before Devlin and placed a hand on his neck. He pushed Devlin's body down onto the floor and Devlin no longer had the strength to resist.

"This, Father, is your destiny. I am here to bring you peace. You have a demon within you, Father Devlin. I am here to separate it from you, and we both know that although your soul will survive, your body will not."

Deeney's hands tightened around Devlin's neck. He placed his other hand on Devlin's chest. The chanting began again, growing very quickly in intensity and wildness.

Deeney began to chant Psalm Sixty-Eight in Latin and, from within his torn innards, Devlin felt something stir. Something that had lived with him for almost three years. The spirit that Felix Lemus, the murderer of his wife and unborn child, had placed in him and named Azazel. As Devlin's life waned the demon within him waxed, growing larger and more extraordinary. Through blurred eyes, Devlin could see Deeney's face. His eyes were closed and his concentration was absolute, as if he were not only trying to draw out, but also attempting to comprehend the demon within Devlin.

The chanting had degraded into howls and groans.

"Don't..." whispered Devlin. "Don't do it..."

Deeney stopped chanting. He looked at Devlin pitifully. "You are as a child. I am your protector and savior... I even know your demon's name... Azazel..."

"You don't understand what you're doing..."

Deeney shut his eyes and continued his invocation.

Suddenly Devlin's being was gripped with the overwhelming sense of something splitting. Cleaving. A profound schism.

Deeney released Devlin abruptly and his eyes opened wide. White smoke was emanating from the wound in Devlin's chest. Both men stared in wonder at the thin fumes climbing from Devlin's body up into the cave air. It was so faint that Devlin wondered if it were only mist. A damp cave mist.

Yet, whatever it was or wasn't, it was growing larger. In moments it was a cloud and then the cloud began to take a shape. A spectral shape that overshadowed Deeney and Devlin. The two men were paralyzed by amazement. The spectral shape-shifted again and seemed to settle into the form of a goat. But a goat with sentient eyes. Wicked eyes.

Devlin knew it wasn't only he and Deeney who could see the form. He knew the others could see it too. He knew because the chanting had stopped and the cave was silent.

Deeney scrambled backward and clutched the crucifix hanging from his neck. He began praying maniacally.

For a moment it was just Devlin and the demon together. Azazel. Maybe Devlin even saw Lemus again, maybe he didn't. But he was suddenly, absolutely, certain that the shape above him, that had climbed out of his body, was offering him a choice. The demon could go if Devlin wanted. It should have been a simple decision.

But instead of relief, Devlin felt the most enormous and unbearable pity for this beast. Azazel, the scapegoat, the outcast. And maybe the pity was self-pity too. For all that he had lost and the loneliness he had chosen. He also understood that his past, his mistakes, his pain, they were his gravity. His imperfections and sin bound him to this earth and gave him substance. Heaviness.

So, he allowed the demon back inside. Where he belonged. Where he was safe.

44

The only noise in the cave was Deeney's feeble voice in prayer. His eyes were closed. The other men were on their knees, opened mouthed. Lopez was still lying crooked and unconscious on the ground.

Devlin felt his chest. A wound was still there but it wasn't so large, so bloody, so grave. The life that seeped from him had returned.

Strength came back to him with miraculous speed. He found he could stand. He picked up the knife that Deeney had left lying on the floor and walked toward Jamie, who was still cowering under the table.

"You've lost a lot of blood. Can you walk?" asked Devlin.

Jamie nodded. "If you can walk, I can."

Devlin almost laughed.

He took Jamie's hand and they walked unsteadily toward the iron door. Nobody, Deeney included, dared approach them.

Up above ground it was very early morning. Peaceful, too. The kind of peace only the twilight brings. A peace that is profoundly healing. If you let it.

But the peace was broken by the sound of sirens approaching. In a few minutes, Devlin and Jamie were surrounded by squad cars. Cardinal Hermes and Sarah emerged from one of the cars and ran to them.

"Are you okay?" asked Sarah.

"No. Not really," said Devlin.

EPILOGUE

Ten years late, the day of Stephen Martin's funeral finally arrived. The air was sharp like cold pins and the sunlight came down hard and slanting. A bright, fierce January day. All four boys were to be given funerals at Holy Cross. Stephen's would be the first of them. The only living relation to attend was Sarah, but even so, the church was full to brimming with townspeople, and some cable news reporters too.

Devlin took the service and Sarah gave a reading. Then they processed out into the cemetery where Stephen was finally laid to rest.

Later, when the crowds and news crews had dispersed, Sarah and Devlin took time to stand by the grave. Just the two of them.

The headstone was simple. "Stephen James Martin. March 1997 - January 2012. Rest in Peace."

"It feels like more than Stephen was put to rest today," said Sarah, shivering from the wind despite her heavy wool coat. "I feel like I'm at peace too."

"I know what you mean," replied Devlin.

The afternoon sky had gotten hazier and sunlight came and went as clouds passed over.

"The mystic was right," Sarah continued. "There was someone else inside me. Trying to get through. It was Stephen."

"She definitely saw something. I'd have to give her some credit. I still wouldn't advise going to a mystic though," Devlin replied dubiously.

Sarah laughed. She seemed to find Devlin's serious reply amusing. Devlin turned to Sarah and smiled. The winter sun was shifting fast, and light and shadow played about Sarah's face and body. Devlin suddenly had the notion that something fundamental about Sarah had changed, though he couldn't put his finger on what it was.

"What's wrong?" asked Sarah. "You look a bit freaked out."

Devlin thought twice about saying anything, but they had been through so much. "Maybe it's my imagination, but something about you is different."

Sarah smiled enigmatically. "Maybe something is."

"Wait... Are you...?"

"Yes...I am."

"Wow... Well, congratulations."

"Thank you. So, you're not shocked? About me not being married?"

"You'll make a great mom. That's what's important. Does Tom know?"

"Not yet. I'll tell him. In the meantime, I'll move back to Mom's. I don't want to go back with Tom. He's not who I thought he was. I want to have this child and raise it, and Tom can be a part of that... If he wants. This child is wanted. Like Stephen should have been wanted."

Sarah shook her head in wonder. "Maybe that's why it all happened. The mystic and Stephen's body being found. Maybe it was the force of life. Maybe Amber Luna saw a new life in me as well as an old life."

They stood in silence for a moment, the wind and sun passing over them. Snow was starting to fall and looked like it would settle.

"You never wanted children," said Sarah. "That's what you said. I don't think that's true, is it?"

"No. It's not. Some years ago I was married and my wife was pregnant. But they both died."

"How?"

"They were shot."

"My God. I'm so sorry..." Sarah reached out and held Devlin's hand, falling silent in thought for a moment. Then she said, "Had you given your child a name?"

The question shook Devlin. He'd told several people about his wife and child, but no one had asked him if there was a name. The funny thing was, they had settled on a name. Somehow, in all the time that had passed, he'd nearly forgotten that they had.

"We did. He was called Michael."

"Well," said Sarah with conviction, "if it's a boy, that's the name my child will have. Will you be around to be part of Michael's life?"

"If you're asking me if I'll stay in Avery, the answer is, I don't know. Before I came here I wasn't a free man. I was carrying a weight with me. But whatever Deeney did to me had unintended consequences. I feel freer now than I have done in some time. I even feel... redeemed. I haven't yet made up my mind what that means for the future."

"I'd like you to stay." Sarah placed a hand on her stomach. "We'd like you to stay."

"Well now," said Devlin. "I'd need to stay to do the baptism at least. Because young Michael will grow up a good Catholic boy if I have anything to do with it."

"Let's not jump the gun, shall we? Anyway, can you baptize a baby if the mom's, uh, like me? I mean, out of wedlock?"

"I can if I have a founded hope the baby will be brought up in the Catholic Faith."

Sarah offered an arm and Devlin took it. "Like I say, let's not jump the gun."

Then they walked back to the rectory discussing plans for a new life, while the ground grew white around them.

THE END.

AFTERWORD

Thanks for reading The Last Man. If you want to get the latest news and updates then click on the link to subscribe to my newsletter...

http://eepurl.com/gdVyyX

Regards,

James.

Printed in Great Britain
by Amazon